Ellie Darkins spent her formative years devouring romance novels and, after completing her English degree, decided to make a living from her love of books. As a writer and editor, she finds her work now entails dreaming up romantic proposals, hot dates with alpha males and trips to the past with dashing heroes. When she's not working she can usually be found running around after her toddler, volunteering at her local library or escaping all of the above with a good book and a vanilla latte.

Also by Ellie Darkins

Frozen Heart, Melting Kiss
Bound by a Baby Bump
Newborn on Her Doorstep
Holiday with the Mystery Italian
Falling for the Rebel Princess
Conveniently Engaged to the Boss
Surprise Baby for the Heir

Discover more at millsandboon.co.uk.

FALLING AGAIN FOR HER ISLAND FLING

ELLIE DARKINS

MILLS & BOON

Published in Great Britain 2019
by Mills & Boon, an imprint of HarperCollins*Publishers*
1 London Bridge Street, London, SE1 9GF

© 2019 Ellie Darkins

ISBN: 978-0-263-08089-6

MIX
Paper from
responsible sources
FSC™ C007454

This book is produced from independently certified FSC™ paper
to ensure responsible forest management.
For more information visit www.harpercollins.co.uk/green.

Printed and bound in Great Britain
by CPI Group (UK) Ltd, Croydon, CR0 4YY

For my girls

CHAPTER ONE

MEENA LAY ON her back, the sand hot beneath her, the sun reaching her face through the leaves of the coconut trees, and breathed deeply, grateful for the shade even this early in the morning. By lunchtime the heat would be fierce, and she would be forced indoors, so she really should be making the most of her time here on the island of Le Bijou before she had to get back to the St Antoine mainland. But lying on the beach, alone in the sunlight, was still something of a dream. Especially here. Something that she had imagined for so long. Had started to fear would never happen again. It was something she could never take for granted.

She took another breath, long and slow, relaxing her body from the tips of her fingers down to her toes. It was still a marvel that she could make it follow her commands so easily, after the years that she had spent relearning how to use it. It had taken more strength than she'd known she had to get her body working again after the accident, and still more for her to be able to face the world and reintegrate herself into real life.

From the outside now one would never guess what

had happened to her. Her thick dark hair, worn in its natural curls, did a perfect job of hiding the scars on her head. Her standard-issue Environmental Agency polo shirt or a wetsuit over a one-piece swimsuit took care of the rest.

But the scars were still there. She could feel them on her scalp and her body. Feel them in her mind, every time that she tried to recall the months before the accident and found them blank. And then there were the looks and the whispers that she knew followed her around the island. She was the girl who had been hit by a car and lost her mind.

The dappled light grew darker behind her eyelids and she blinked them open, uneasy. She sat up quickly as she realised she was right to be concerned. A man was standing over her, casting a shadow where she had been lying in the sand. With the sun behind him, she couldn't make out his features, and she scrambled to her feet, heart tripping a little faster, glancing around her to see if there was anyone about who might hear her if she had to call out for help.

'Meena?' the man asked, sounding as if he was choking on her name.

'Do I know you?' she replied in English, picking up on his Australian accent even in that one word. Like most residents of St Antoine, an island nation in the Indian Ocean, she was fluent in the French the islanders used every day as well as English, the official language of government business, and of course the colourful creole that the islanders used amongst themselves. But she'd lived in Australia for a year while she'd been at university and the accent never failed to tug at her heart.

She narrowed her eyes, looking at him closely. Was there something familiar about him? She felt as if his name and the memory of who he was were right on the verge of making it into a functional part of her brain. But her brain didn't make the leap, so she launched into her well-rehearsed spiel, the words that she'd carefully formulated over the years to smooth this very social awkwardness.

'I'm sorry if we've met before,' she said, scrambling to her feet while she went through the speech. 'I suffered a head injury and lost some memories.'

She didn't even feel embarrassed any more, she realised, about giving her usual excuse when she didn't recognise someone but got the sense that she probably should. It happened rarely these days. Most of the people whom she'd met and forgotten that summer either knew about her accident already or had just been holidaying on the island and she need never worry about seeing them again. She had spent almost her whole life on St Antoine, the beautiful magnet for tourists and the developers who followed them. But most of the people who stayed here were on once-in-a-lifetime trips and would never know that she had completely forgotten meeting them. It had been a few months, at least, since she had had to make her slightly unorthodox introduction.

The man held out his hand to shake hers, still watching her with trepidation. Probably worried that she was going to fall into a fit or something, she told herself. She'd waited out the five-year danger period after her accident, desperate to get back to diving, her career and her life on hold until she could get back into the water; wondering every day whether this would be the one when a seizure struck. But it had never happened, and she had got herself recertified to dive and back to her conservation work on the island.

'Guy Williams,' he introduced himself. 'I'm—'

'The owner of the development company.' She'd received an email telling her that she should expect him tomorrow, yet here he was, interrupting her relaxation practice a day early.

'You've lost your memories?' he said, still looking at her strangely. Meena rolled her eyes; she used to get this a lot.

'Yes, just like in a movie. Should I remember something about you?'

He shook his head. He was taking this even worse than most people she told. Generally, people just looked puzzled but, even though Guy Williams was a stranger, she could tell from his expression that he was struggling to accept what she'd just revealed. Maybe he didn't believe her.

'Then this is a fresh start,' Meena said, eager to move the conversation along. 'I expect you want to know about the environmental impact assessment. I wasn't expecting you until tomorrow but I was just about to get started.' She glanced around, looking for her clipboard, sure that she had brought it out with her. Oh, way to make a good impression, she thought. Introduce herself with a side note about a brain injury and then look around the beach as if you have no idea what you're doing there.

She was not usually so distracted by a pretty face—even one as pretty as this. High forehead, golden tan, long, straight nose, full lips, a hint of a cleft in his chin. The body wasn't half bad either—she supposed, if she were absolutely pressed to give her opinion on the subject—from what she could see of it, anyway.

He was dressed for business in a conservative shirt and navy suit. But his collar was open, showing just a hint of his throat and making her want to lean closer, to let her fingers drift into that notch, feel the heat of his skin, the throb of his pulse beneath her fingers.

She shook her head. Where had that thought come from? She took a step away from him. She should *not* be thinking that way. She did *not* want a man in her life. She crossed her arms over her chest, suddenly feeling cold despite the growing heat of the day. She'd proved to herself a long time ago that she wasn't capable of making good decisions about men. About sex. It was safer to deny herself either rather than risk repeating her mistakes.

'Are you okay?' Guy asked.

'I'm fine, thank you. I was just about to begin.'

Ah, there. She spotted the clipboard from the corner of her eye and scooped it up in a single, easy movement that belied the many months of physio she'd endured after her accident to enable her to take even a single step.

She caught him looking at her from the corner of her eye and momentarily stopped. 'Are you sure we didn't meet…before?' she asked, hating the black hole in her memory that made the question necessary. She shouldn't have to look at every man she met and ask herself, *Was it you? Was it your baby I was carrying?*

He gave her a look so bland that she knew it couldn't possibly have been him. It was as if he barely saw her at all. As if she were barely *there* at all. Well, she supposed that answered her question well enough.

'I'm sure,' he said with firm politeness. Another one to strike off the list, she thought, trying not to cringe at this internal game of 'who's the daddy?' that she had been forced to play for the last seven years.

She could let it rest, of course. There was no baby. Not now. When she had eventually woken from the coma, the doctors in the clinic had broken it to her gently that it hadn't just been her memories that she'd lost. She didn't even know if she'd known before the accident that she'd been pregnant. Given the conservative attitude to premarital sex across almost every culture on St Antoine, she was sure that an unplanned pregnancy would have been more cause for anxiety than celebrations.

She still remembered the whispers that had followed a school friend who had fallen pregnant in her late teens, and who had hastily been married before the baby arrived six months later. Was that why Meena's lover had disappeared? Had he feared he would be forced into a shotgun wedding? Tied to a woman he didn't love?

Her parents were hardly traditional, though. They had raised eyebrows with their own marriage—

Meena's French-Mauritian mother and Hindu father had married at a time when such relationships had been even more unusual than they were now—but that didn't mean that people wouldn't talk. They always talked.

She had been unusual too in living away from her parents: it had taken every ounce of determination she'd had to move out when she'd been sufficiently recovered from her accident.

But if her family knew about any boyfriend she'd had they had never said anything. So she had no choice but to assume that the relationship had been a secret. How could she have been serious enough about someone to have slept with him but not serious enough to introduce him to her parents?

Her mind had spent many hours tying itself in knots trying to work it out. She hadn't been far along and what worried her the most was that she had no idea who the father could have been. She was only missing a few months of memory, and there had been no sign of a boyfriend in her life, so where had this baby come from—and what had happened to the father? Where had he been when she'd been trapped under that car, her memories and their baby leaving her body?

Leaving her broken.

Guy turned to look back up the beach to the scrubland where the hotel complex would be built. Where it *could* be built, Meena corrected herself, as long as the environmental studies were clear and planning permission was granted by the relevant government department. If she couldn't find something to hold up the development… She took a deep breath. She would find something—she had to—because there was something about this tiny jewel of an island on which she wasn't going to give up.

For seven years it had felt like her secret. In all the trauma and recovery of that time, she had spent more time here, at this secluded beach, than just about anywhere else. It was the only place where she felt still. At peace. Where her mind rested and her heart didn't hurt. So when she had heard about the upcoming development she had made sure that she was on the environmental impact team. If there was any way of stopping the resort from being built, then she was going to be the one to find it.

Meena Bappoo. Flat-backed on the beach, just as he'd left her. Eyes closed to the sun, as if it had been minutes since he had last seen her here rather than years. He'd nearly turned and walked away when he'd seen the Environmental Agency logo on her shirt and realised she was the agency marine biologist he was meant to be meeting. The notes that he'd received from his project manager's schedule hadn't mentioned her by name, only her job title and the time and location of the meeting, though it turned out that he had mixed up the date.

And then her lids had snapped open, he'd seen those warm golden-brown eyes again and he'd known he was too entranced to walk away.

Did he believe her story? Her memory loss seemed far-fetched. But she hadn't really given him a choice:

he had to believe her. The way she'd looked at him was so completely blank. Surely she couldn't have been so unmoved if she'd remembered even a moment of those few months that they'd spent together?

Because he remembered. He remembered *everything*. The way that she spoke, her island creole accent that he knew could slip so quickly into perfect French or her slightly American-sounding English. The way that she smelled—of salt, sand and the coconut oil that she rubbed into her skin. The way that she had looked at him after they had made love for the first time, as if they had just created the stars in the sky.

The way that he had waited for her as they'd agreed, after he had returned to Australia, and she had never shown up.

Had it been the accident? he wondered now. That would make sense, answer the questions he had been carrying around in the years since they had been together. It hit him like a blow to the chest, the thought that perhaps he had been wrong. That she had wanted to come as desperately as he had wanted it. But it didn't hurt any less when she looked at him and didn't *see* him.

He'd thought of her over the years. Thought of *them*. Thought of the days and the nights that they had spent on this beach. Thought of the night, years later, that he'd made the decision to buy the tiny uninhabited island of Le Bijou and build his resort. Thought of the pain that he had felt when he had been left alone, wanting her, wondering what had gone wrong. Thought of all the ways that he had tried to numb that pain, and the consequences that had spiralled out of control.

And then he couldn't think about it any more, because the loss and grief from that time of his life was still too painful, too raw even to glance at, never mind examine more closely.

He'd come here to get over her. To face their past, bury it, landscape over the evidence and then move on. But then he'd seen her lying there, looking exactly as she had the day that he'd left her, and known immediately that it was a mistake.

But maybe the fact she didn't remember him was a saving grace. She had no idea what they'd once shared and he had every intention of keeping things that way. He could never let her know what they had been to one another. What he had felt for her. He'd spent years trying to get over her. To shake the pain that her rejection had caused him. And he couldn't bear to reopen those old wounds. Not now.

They were over. They had been over for a long time. She didn't even remember that they had ever been together and, as far as he could see, that was a good thing. He wouldn't take that away from her and replace it with the anger and bile that had built up and then been fought down over the years. If she knew what he had done—who he had become—after the last time he had left this island she could only be relieved that she had escaped him.

It was kinder to lie, he told himself, convincing himself of its truth. He had to live with what they had lost and he wouldn't wish that on her too. Not now, when he knew that he could never again be that person he had been when they'd been together. Even though they were here on Le Bijou, they could never go back and be who they had been before.

He couldn't risk being in a relationship again. The only time he had tried it since Meena had ended in the worst possible way, and it was something for which he would never forgive himself. There was no way that he could ever let Meena get involved with him again. She was better off without him. Better off not knowing him.

Meena turned and looked at him, and he knew he'd been caught staring. He couldn't let that happen, he chastised himself. Couldn't let her see what he felt for her—what he *had* felt for her, he corrected—those long years ago. Before she'd failed to turn up as she'd promised and confirmed what he'd always known about himself—what his parents had made clear for as long as he could remember—that he just wasn't worth it.

She'd never let him become part of her life here on the island. Or vice versa. He'd agreed to it at the time because, more than anything, he'd just wanted her in his life and the sneaking around had felt fun at first. But he had realised, later, that she had done it on purpose, had kept their relationship separate from the rest of her life, so that when it was over she could move on.

He wouldn't let it happen again because they were done. She had no idea they'd ever started anything in the first place and that was a blessing.

'So I'm going to make a start on the detailed environmental impact study tomorrow,' Meena said eventually. 'You should have already received the initial report; this one will go into greater detail on the areas that were raised as a concern. I'll keep you updated with the results as I progress.'

'Do that,' Guy replied shortly, wanting this meeting at an end. 'I need those permissions in place as soon as possible if I'm going to keep to my schedule.' And he *would* be keeping to his schedule and leaving as quickly as possible. If his usual project manager hadn't broken his thigh bone in a nasty jet-ski accident, Guy wouldn't have had to take this meeting. He would have been on the island and off again within a couple of days, leaving everything in the capable hands of his team. It was the only way that he had been able to contemplate being back here at all, to minimise the risk of accidentally bumping into Meena. Now he was faced with the prospect of managing this himself, for the foreseeable future at least, and that meant managing Meena. Or trying to. He couldn't think that he had ever been successful at it before.

'Well, don't think I will rush it,' Meena said right on cue, confirming his fears of how this working relationship was going to proceed. 'There are reefs on this side of the island and the coral is very vulnerable. It's my responsibility to make sure that the environment isn't harmed by your building developments here, and I'm not going to cut corners. If you want to build here, you have to take care of the island first.'

He gritted his teeth, knowing that his tension was probably showing on his face. But why hide it? She didn't care what he was thinking. He was nothing to her. A stranger.

'I understand that—I think my plans have made reasonable provisions for the environment, so there should be no hold-ups. I will be following your work closely.'

She bristled at that, crossing her arms and fixing him with a glare. Good. He could handle her like this. He could handle angry. Angry was nothing like what he remembered between them. Angry didn't bring back memories that still—somehow—had the power to hurt him. Well, not for much longer. Once his plans were under way, this island would no longer be recognisable. Would no longer call to him. Would no longer be the yardstick by which he unconsciously measured his experiences and his relationships. Of course, no *real* woman could live up to an island fantasy, a summer romance with a beautiful girl while he'd been on holiday, barely into his twenties.

'Where are you going to start with your report?' he asked, trying to read her notes upside down. But her notes were in French. A language he had started to learn once—with scribbled love notes—here, with her—but had fallen out of using. Another very good reason he had hired a capable project manager to oversee this development. As soon as he got off this tiny island and back to the capital, he would be instructing his assistant, Dev, to find a temporary replacement for his injured project manager.

'I need to inspect the reef,' Meena said, checking her list. 'Many of the ones nearby have suffered from coral bleaching or damage from boats, and my initial look showed that these reefs appeared to be suffering similarly. At the very least we would need to do any remedial work before building is approved and make a plan for how it can be protected from further human damage. My other main concern is the turtle population. I saw tracks on the beach that indicate there may be a nesting site. We need to wait out the incubation period to see what, if anything, hatches, and to ensure that increased use of the beach won't impact on breeding or migratory patterns.'

He nodded, wondering how much time this was all going to take. But these were details, and he was no longer the details guy. He was the money and he was the vision. One of the joys of being the boss of your own multi-billion-dollar resort business was letting someone else worry about the bloody turtles.

'I'm sure your report will be fine, Miss Bappoo. Just submit your findings to my office and someone will be in touch.'

He turned away from her but then stopped, his feet halting in the sand. Was this it? Was it all finally going to end with a glib remark about turtles? With Meena having no idea that they had met before today? He turned back and looked at her. Really looked. He saw pink rise in her cheeks at his unmasked appraisal of her.

Seven years. That was how long it had been since he had seen her. And yet he couldn't see any sign of it on her face. Her cheeks, rosy beneath the warm bronze-brown of her skin, were still the smooth apples that he remembered. Her eyes were as golden and as full of challenge as they had been then.

What would she think of him, he wondered, if she remembered the man—boy—he had been? Would she find him much changed? His body was no softer—he had worked hard to ensure that. His heart, however, was harder—she was responsible for that. He shook his head. That wasn't fair. He couldn't entirely blame her for the way he had behaved after they had broken up. He had to carry that alone.

He held her gaze for a moment longer. He needed to know that she had seen him—really seen him. To give her one last chance to recognise him. To remember.

The blush faded from her cheeks as he refused to look away and her expression changed. He didn't know her well enough any more to guess what she was thinking. But in that moment it wasn't indifference. Curiosity, maybe. Desire. Did he want that? Would this feel better if she wanted him? If he was the one to walk away this time? Probably not, he conceded.

Anyway, those wounds had healed a long time ago, he told himself. He didn't need them to be reopened. 'So, goodbye, then,' he said, and turned from her, walking back towards his speedboat, knowing this would be the last time that he saw her. It had to be.

CHAPTER TWO

'COME IN.'

Guy glanced at the schedule on the computer monitor; he wasn't expecting a meeting and the knock on the door had taken him by surprise. In fact, he hadn't been expecting still to be on the island at all, but the search for a replacement project manager was proving to be more difficult than he had hoped. He'd already delayed his departure from the island by a fortnight, and the replacement that he'd hired couldn't fly out for another week at the earliest. Guy was going to have to get the environmental permissions he needed before he could get back to Sydney. Whoever was at the door had better be quick. He had three days' worth of work to do that evening. The last thing he needed was an unscheduled five o'clock meeting.

In the promotional brochures he'd had mocked up, he'd billed his island as paradise. But most of what he'd seen of the country in the last two weeks was the inside of its government buildings and his air-conditioned office. He could have been in the offices of any of his corporate buildings for all he'd seen of the local environment.

The door opened and he glanced up; his body registered her presence before his brain did. Before her name formed on his lips, his heart was beating wildly in his chest and there was a tightness, low in his belly, that seemed a response unique to being close to her.

'Meena, what are you doing here?'

Way to play it cool, he chastised himself, angry that she still had that hold over him, the ability to make him say what he was thinking without any regard for whether it was a good idea. When they'd been younger, it had felt like a blessing: their mutual honesty helping them past the barrier of dive instructor and pupil. Past the social conventions of a conservative culture and into the realms of something much more personal.

'Your environmental reports,' she replied, her brow furrowed into a curious expression. 'I emailed them over to Dev and he told me you'd want me to come and talk through my findings in person.'

'And why is that?' he asked, wondering why his assistant had thought that another meeting would be the way to cap off today. 'Never mind. Just give me the highlights.' He leaned back in his chair and folded his arms. The last thing this project needed was more delays.

'Well, the headline is, I'm not giving the approval for your permits.'

Guy sighed, leaned forward again, rested his elbows on his desk and gestured towards the chair opposite, inviting her to take a seat.

'Why not? What's the problem?'

She crossed to his desk and laid out the paperwork in front of him. 'The main problem right now is that the reef won't withstand an increase in boat traffic or sedimentation from the building work. There's been extensive bleaching and it needs to be stabilised and then an ongoing regeneration plan put in place.'

He gritted his teeth. *Ongoing*. 'Ongoing' wasn't a word he wanted to hear in the context of this development, and not from Meena of all people.

'Anything else?'

'There's still no sign of hatchlings from the possible turtle nesting site. We need to wait out the incubation period and see what we're dealing with before I could give the go-ahead.'

'How much time are we looking at?'

'A couple more wee—'

'Unacceptable,' he interrupted. 'This needs to be wrapped up within a week maximum, Miss Bappoo. I can't leave the island until they're done, and I need to get back to Sydney.'

'With all due respect, that isn't for you to say,' she replied, crossing her arms. 'This will take as long as it takes. It's not something you hurry. It's not something you *can* hurry. This is my call.'

He looked at her, assessing. Was she doing this on purpose? he wondered. Because of their past? And then he had to remind himself that she didn't even remember their past. She wasn't angry with him. She didn't feel *anything* for him. He envied her ignorance. He wished that he could see this as she undoubtedly did: a simple business matter with no personal feelings involved.

'That's not good enough,' he stated, leaning back in his chair.

She mirrored him, implacable. He remembered that look and he knew that it meant that there was no changing her mind. 'Unfortunately for you, your feelings on the matter aren't a criterion in my report.'

He shook his head. A standoff wasn't going to get them anywhere fast. Cooperation was the only way that he was going to get this project moving again. 'Tell me what I can do to make this happen faster.'

He saw his more relaxed demeanour soften her. 'You can stop asking questions like that for a start,' Meena said. 'Faster isn't the aim here; environmental conservation is. I'm not letting this island come to harm because you want to throw your hotel up *faster.*'

'I'm not *throwing* anything,' he retorted. 'And you say that like you think I want to cause harm. I don't; that's why you're here.'

'Good to know. I'll note it in the report.'

He paused. 'Meena, I...'

She was doing all this to protect the island. *Their* island. The tiny speck of sand and rock in the Indian Ocean. Could it be that she remembered it? That that was why she was being so fiercely protective of it? The thought warmed him somewhere deep but he shook off the feeling. That wasn't what this was about. She didn't remember him. She didn't remember anything about who they had been to each other.

'Look,' Guy said. 'I want this application to go

through and I have no interest in doing any harm to Le Bijou,' he lied. 'Tell me what I need to do to make that happen.'

She narrowed her eyes as she looked at him. 'You really want to do this right?'

He nodded. 'I really do.'

'Then you need a marine biologist on your team once building starts. Someone to ensure you are considering environmental impacts at every stage. You need short-term and long-term sustainability plans, and someone to hold you to account.'

He gave an ironic smile. 'You seem to be doing a pretty good job of that.'

'For now.' She smiled back. 'But my job's done when the reports are completed. This island needs a permanent guardian.'

'You're right. And you're perfect for the job.'

As he said the words he knew that it was true. Much as he hated to admit it, she would be the perfect person to make sure that the island was protected through the building of the resort, and after. And once his new project manager started he would be gone and he wouldn't have to see her again. If this was what it took to get the permits approved, he would do it. He could see from her face that she was surprised by the offer nonetheless.

'I have a job,' she said abruptly.

'True.' He shrugged. 'But here's the offer of another. Because you're right. An in-house marine biologist should always have been a part of the plan. I think this offer shows how serious I am about getting these permits. Your report proves you know what you're doing. And you love the island.' He knew what love looked like on her. He had seen it before. He remembered lying on that beach, seeing her look at him and knowing—*knowing*—that she loved him. He didn't know what he'd done to deserve it then. He knew that he didn't deserve it now.

Which was why it was such a spectacularly bad idea to offer her the job. He should be putting as much distance between them as he could right now. Not creating yet another bond.

It was fine, he reminded himself. As soon as he had a replacement project manager in place, he would be leaving this island and not coming back. In his headquarters in Sydney, he would have no more contact with Meena than with thousands of his other employees and contractors. She wouldn't be his problem any more. Wouldn't be in his life any more.

'I'll have to think about it,' she replied slowly, as if looking for the catch in his offer.

She could do a lot for Le Bijou as the resident marine biologist, Meena acknowledged, turning Guy's job offer over in her mind. She had done a lot of good when she had worked at another resort before her accident, she reminded herself, educating holidaymakers and divers about the local area and how to dive without impacting the coral reefs. She had even started a programme of coral regeneration with newlyweds, planting out coral, something that would carry on growing long after the honeymoon was over.

She could do the same at Le Bijou, she thought, if she took up Guy's job offer. She could stay on the island. Do her best for it. Protect it as best she could once the works were completed and the worst of the damage had been done.

Perhaps damage limitation was all she *could* do. Guy owned Le Bijou, and it was going to change. Her sanctuary. It just wouldn't exist any more. Not in the way that she wanted—needed—it to.

But something made her hesitate before telling Guy that she wanted the job. Working with Guy, specifically, made her hesitate.

She'd thought a lot about men the last few years. A lot about specifically what sort of man would make her fall for him. She knew she wouldn't have slept with someone she didn't love. Last she remembered, she had been a virgin planning to wait until she was married, as was expected of her. And then she was waking from a coma, finding out that she had been pregnant, and the only clues she had to her mystery boyfriend were notes she'd found months after she had finally left the clinic, scribbled in French on the back of a dive planner.

I love you. I can't wait to see you again. Meet me at our beach.

She had wondered ever since then who he could have been. Who her type was. What sort of man she had fallen in love with.

And now here was Guy and the strange sense of

déjà vu she felt around him. It was probably just his accent, she thought. The twang of his Australian vowels
that was so familiar from her scholarship year studying there. That was what was giving her this strange
feeling, she decided. There was no way that Guy was
her mystery boyfriend. The way that he looked at her
was so cold, so impersonal, it couldn't possibly be him.

Which made the dreams she had been having about
him all the stranger. They felt so vivid, so real. She had
touched him. Smelled him. Tasted him. In her sleep
last night she had run her fingertips over every part
of his body and then followed them with her tongue.
He had spanned her waist with his hands, cupped the
curve of her hip and her buttock, teased her with his
lips.

All of which was making this meeting extremely
awkward.

She risked another glance up at him, but his eyes
were still fixed on his computer screen.

'I want to know what working with you will mean.'

'I'm glad you're considering it.' He didn't look as
if he thought it was great. Considering he'd made the
offer in the first place, he looked as if he didn't want
her there at all. Well, it was too late. She'd been thinking about Le Bijou. What it would mean to stand guard
over it. However awkward things got with Guy.

'Are you sure we haven't met before?'

She wasn't really aware of thinking the question
before it popped out of her mouth. He was just so…
unsettling. He unnerved her. And she couldn't help
thinking that there must be a reason he had this effect

on her. Must be a reason why her body reacted to him every time that he was close. A reason her heart was racing and her palms were sweating.

Was it you? Her mind jumped to the familiar question. *Did you love me? Did I carry your baby? Lose your baby?*

He sighed, looked up and made eye contact with her for the first time since she had walked into the room.

'What period of time are you missing memories from?' he asked. 'I've only visited St Antoine once before.'

She told him the date of her accident, and that she didn't remember the three months before, wondering at the change in his demeanour.

'I was here then,' he said. 'My parents own the Williams resort on the mainland. I was staying there for the summer.'

'But I worked there!' Meena exclaimed. 'I was working at the dive school before my accident. It was the summer after I got back from Australia,' she added, realising she'd never mentioned to him that connection. Was this the reason for his strangeness? For the strange familiarity she felt around him? Would she have mentioned that if she'd bumped into an Australian guest? Would she have struck up a conversation about that common link?

'So maybe I have seen you before, or maybe we spoke back then? I'm sorry,' she added, realising she was speaking out loud. 'It's just, it's hard, having this gap in my memories. It makes me question myself. Question what I know, you know?'

Of course he didn't know. How could he? How could anyone know what it felt like to live in a body and a mind that didn't fully belong to them?

'Maybe we did meet.' Guy shuffled some papers on his desk, not looking at her. 'I went to the dive school when I was here before. Maybe we crossed paths.'

'But you don't remember? You don't remember me?' It was clear from the way that he had turned back to his work that he was ready for this meeting to be over. But it had been so long since she had had any new information about that time that she couldn't let this drop, no matter how annoying Guy seemed to be finding her.

Just once in her life, she wanted a straightforward answer. No, scratch that. Once in her life she wanted to know the answer to questions about her life herself, without relying on near strangers to fill in the gaps. But as that didn't seem to be an option, no matter what she or her medical team had tried, she would have to settle for getting answers from someone else. For trusting other people to paint this picture of who she had been.

'I don't remember you,' Guy said, looking back at his screen. 'I'm sorry.'

'No need to be sorry.' Meena shrugged, tried to cover her disappointment. No answers, again. No reason for why she felt this strange familiarity around Guy. For him and for Le Bijou.

'Get in touch with Dev about the details of the new job, if you want to consider it. And keep him updated with your progress on the environmental reports. If there's nothing else...'

It was clear she was being dismissed.

'Okay, great.' She forced professionalism back into her voice. 'Well, I'm going to go have another look at the reef tomorrow. To see if there is any way that its decline can be reversed, or at least halted. If you want to come and see for yourself, you would be welcome.'

Guy glanced up at her, meeting her gaze again. Maybe this was why he avoided it, Meena thought, as she felt her cheeks warm under his scrutiny. Maybe he could see the effect he had on her when he turned his full attention on her like that. No wonder he didn't want to encourage it.

'I'll see what I can do. But I have a very full week.'

Did he remember her? Only every night in his dreams, in waking moments when his mind wandered, and for a moment he was back there, the sun and her lips on his body once again. He remembered everything.

And it broke him, almost daily now.

Because whatever, wherever they were now, they were never going to get that back. What they had had back then had been beautiful. It had been pure. It had been innocent. And then the darkness in his heart when he'd thought that she had abandoned him had sullied it. And that simply couldn't be undone.

He must have been broken before he had even met her, for that rot to have set in and cause the damage that it had.

If he told her what they had shared, what would she think of that? What could she take from it? Worst-case scenario, she would want to try to turn back time. To see what had brought them together then. To see if it still existed.

She had lost all the time that they had been together. He had spent three months on this island, ostensibly getting to know his family's resort on the St Antoine mainland as preparation for a formal role in the company. But in truth he had spent most of it getting to know Meena. His parents hadn't even been disappointed when they'd realised how little work he'd done that summer. As if they'd been expecting his failure all along. It was so easy to disappoint them, he realised, when they had such low expectations of him.

Meena thought that she wanted to know him, but she was wrong. The only possible outcome was her getting hurt, and he could spare her that at least.

Of course, his heart had hurt when he'd seen how lost she was without those memories. And he could fix that, he knew. He could tell her everything, and she wouldn't have to worry and guess at what had happened in those months.

But would that help her, really? To know that she had been in love with a man who didn't exist any more? No, it was kinder to say nothing, he told himself. Kinder—and safer—that she never knew what they had once had, and what they had both lost.

CHAPTER THREE

WHY HAD SHE invited him? Meena asked herself for the millionth time that day. It had been a stupid idea at the time, and felt even stupider now that she was sitting in her boat, in a rash-guard swimsuit and shorts, wondering if he was going to show up.

Of course he wasn't. He had been awkward and uncomfortable for the entirety of their short acquaintance, so he was hardly going to be signing up for extracurriculars. And no wonder, considering the way that she had quizzed him the last time that they had met, making a near stranger uncomfortable by trying to use his memories to patch together her defective one. And it had all been for nothing anyway. He hadn't known her then and didn't care now.

She checked over her equipment one more time, including the battery and memory card on her underwater camera. Ideally she needed some close-up shots of the unstable areas of the reef so that she could make a more thorough assessment of whether the damage could be reversed. She was hoping that transplanting in new corals would stabilise it. But if the damage had already gone too far and the reef was starting to crumble she would have to rethink her options. The best way to decide was to get down there for another look. But if Guy didn't show she would have to make do with photographing from the glass-bottomed boat. Even seven years after her accident, when the chance of having a seizure was minimal, she wouldn't risk being out in the water alone.

She needed to choose the best sites for transplanting in the coral pieces she'd retrieved after a storm a few months before, and had been growing out in the lab ever since. If Guy turned up and she had a buddy, then she could get her fins wet and take a closer look.

She looked along the beach, wondering how long she should wait for him, then shook her head; it was time to get to work. She steered her boat over to the reef, anchored carefully in the white sand, taking care not to damage the reef, and pulled out her clipboard and her camera, ready to make her observations.

As she took her first shot, she heard the steady buzz of motor. She looked up, shielding her eyes from the fierce morning sun, and spotted the company-branded speedboat rounding the far side of the island. Guy. She took a moment to calm her nerves and gather herself before he stopped on the beach. He didn't know that she was still dreaming about him, and he definitely didn't know about the X-rated images her brain was now happy to summon at will. The light, golden tan of his skin beaded with sweat. His eyes creased with intensity as he moved above her. His body a collection of hard planes that her hands had explored and come to know so well.

In her sleep.

It wasn't real life. And he would never, *ever* find out about those dreams.

The speedboat pulled up to the jetty and she watched Guy climb down the couple of steps to the sand and then look around. He spotted her and gave a brisk wave as she pulled up the anchor and steered back to the shore. Guy came over and helped her to tie the boat to the small wooden jetty. He was dressed more casually than she had seen him before, in cargo shorts and a polo shirt, and she tried to keep her eyes on his face, well away from the extra skin that he was showing.

The last thing her brain needed was new material. It had done quite a good job of conjuring up a naked Guy from just the skin of his hands and his face, and that triangle of his throat where he left his shirt open at the collar. But it turned out her peripheral vision was doing a more than okay job of measuring him up: the golden-blond hair on his forearms that caught the morning sunlight. The strong lines of his calves above his beach shoes. Even his feet seemed familiar. Her brain had been remarkably thorough. And accurate. She had to give herself credit for that.

She must be retrofitting, that was all, she told herself. Her brain was seeing the real thing now and simply slotting the new images into her memories of her fantasies.

Of all the people to be unsurprised by what the human brain could remember and forget, it should be her. Her brain had forgotten everything: who she was, how to walk, how to feed herself. And then it had relearned or remembered almost all of it again. Even with the whole 'missing summer' issues, she couldn't deny being impressed by what she and her brain had achieved between them. Summoning a perfect, naked Guy from just the glimpses she had seen so far proved that various important parts of her were functioning just fine.

She shook her head, trying to dislodge those thoughts before Guy could guess what she was thinking.

'You made it,' she said, offering him her hand to shake, trying to remember to be professional. She simply refused to be affected by the touch of his skin on hers. Nor to remember anything about her dreams inspired by the spark of electricity she felt. She was going to be working with him in her role at the Environmental Agency even if she didn't take up his job offer.

Although, with Guy due to be far away at his Sydney office in a couple of weeks, she barely needed to know that he existed at all in order to do her job. That was for the best, she told herself. Being distracted by a man was in no way a part of her plan for her life. She was here to work, to protect as much of the islands that made up St Antoine as possible, and nothing else.

'Do you have snorkel gear?' she asked Guy, setting a professional tone. 'I have some spares in the lockbox,' she went on, trying to avoid meeting his eye, instead busying herself with equipment and checklists. 'You can stay on the boat if you prefer; see the reef through the glass floor. It's not a bad view from there, and then I can do the underwater stuff.'

'I have my equipment in the boat,' he said shortly.

'Great.' She kept her voice neutral, refusing to react to his brusque tone. There was no reason he should be anything but cold and short with her. They were business colleagues and nothing more, she reminded herself. 'I always prefer to have a buddy in the water, even if I'm only snorkelling.'

'I only have an hour.'

She tried not to bristle again at his tone. She had no reason to court his approval. She didn't want to be his friend. In fact, the more brusque he was with her, the better. The last thing she needed was to think about getting close to this man. Any man, in fact.

She had already proved that she couldn't trust herself to manage her own desires sensibly. In the space of a summer she had met, slept with and then lost her only sexual partner. A man who, it seemed, had been happy to take her to bed but less keen on sticking around after her accident, for her miscarriage or her rehab. If that was the kind of man that she chose for herself, she was better off single. Or even giving in and allowing her aunties to arrange an introduction to someone that fit the older generation's idea of a 'nice young man'.

But that didn't exactly appeal either.

And what nice young man would want her, if they knew? A woman with a brain injury, with the scars of the accident still clear on her body and in her mind.

Who had carried and lost a baby without even knowing who the father was.

She didn't need to worry about that with Guy, at least. He looked at her with disdain, spoke with impatience and was in a hurry to leave the country. He hardly needed warning off. He clearly didn't share the fantasies playing through her mind.

She checked over the equipment that he fetched from the boat. Guy might be experienced, but if he was accompanying her then she would be responsible for his safety, even if it was just a shallow snorkel for the most part. The equipment was top of the range, of course. Far superior to her own snorkel, mask and fins.

She glanced over at him as they both sat on the edge of the boat, steering the way over to where she had anchored by the reef before, and felt a stab of déjà vu. It wasn't an unusual feeling for her; with an injury like hers she was constantly unsure of whether a memory was real or imagined. Before the accident, she would have just shrugged it off. But Guy had piqued her curiosity, telling her that he had attended the dive school when she had been teaching. Could they be sure that they hadn't dived together before? There had to be some reason why she was feeling this way around him.

'What?' Guy asked when he turned and caught her staring at him.

'It's nothing,' she said, creasing her brow, still getting that feeling of déjà vu. Trying to unpack whether there was any truth to the feeling that they had sat like this, on the side of a boat, before.

'Just that…this feels familiar. Us, on a boat like this. It feels like a memory. I'm sorry. It's hard to explain.'

Guy frowned, his forehead lining in what she knew must be a mirror image of her own.

'You remember something?'

'No.' She shook her head. 'I'm sorry. It's not a memory, just a weird feeling. I'm sure it's nothing.' She shrugged, trying to rid herself of the weird sensation. She almost gasped in shock when his hand landed on hers.

'I'm sorry,' he said. 'It must be difficult.' She hadn't been expecting to see empathy in his expression, but there it was. With most people who knew about her amnesia she saw pity. Or gratitude that it had happened to her and not them. But she could see her own pain reflected in Guy's eyes—real understanding—and she didn't know what to make of it.

'It's fine, mostly,' she lied. He didn't need to know the nights she lay awake, trying to force those memories back. Trying to remember who she had been with that summer. And then, maybe, to try to understand who *she* had been that summer. The person who had taken risks. Who had snuck around with a secret lover none of her friends or family knew about. Who'd been stupid enough to fall pregnant with a man who hadn't cared enough to stick around when she'd been hurt.

Guy squeezed her hand and let go, rubbing at the stubble just starting to shadow his jawline. Looking away, she reached over the side of the boat to dip her mask in the water, then slid the strap behind her head and tightened it. It was impossible to be serious with a person wearing a snorkel, and she was counting on that to break the atmosphere that seemed to have grown and thickened between them in the last few moments.

She glanced over and smiled at the sight of Guy in his mask. She was right; not even Guy—as sexy as he was, as vividly sensual as her dreams had been—could carry off that look. He grinned at her in return, and she breathed a sigh of relief.

'Ready?' she asked, and then slipped off the side of the boat and entered the water with a splash. She looked around to make sure Guy had followed her in. He was right behind her, and her body bumped his as she turned. She moved away, dipping under the water, exhaling through her snorkel, leaving a trail of bubbles behind her. His skin on hers was too distracting; she needed to put a sensible amount of space between them. She swam over to the reef, her camera on a tether clipped to her top, and waited for Guy to catch her up. She pointed out the areas where the coral bleaching was at its worst, and then over to the other side of the reef where there was a large unstable section and some damage that looked as if it had been caused by a boat anchor.

This was where she could do the most good. If the bleaching had gone on for so long that the coral had died, that couldn't be reversed, and even if she transplanted new coral into those areas it might suffer the same fate. But over on this side of the reef she had a chance to repair the damage. If she could secure the unstable sections of coral by transplanting in new colonies from other parts of the islands, then it stood a chance of growing back as healthy and vibrant an ecosystem as it had been in the past.

But there were no guarantees. She'd been part of several transplantation efforts over the two years that she'd been back at the Environmental Agency. Some of them had flourished; some of them she'd watched as they'd faded and died, despite every intervention that she could think of to try.

She signed to Guy to let him know what she was doing and dived a little deeper, holding her breath as the end of her snorkel dipped below the water. She took some more photographs, going as deep as she could within the reef without touching the coral and adding to the problems it was facing. She tried to decide if underneath the unstable sections it could support a transplanted colony, and the evidence that she would have to present to the Environmental Agency and to Guy if her plan was going to be approved.

She looked up towards Guy and kicked her legs to come up to the surface. He had stayed near the top of the reef, watching her rather than looking at the coral. There wasn't much of interest on this part of the reef to look at, she acknowledged. With most of the coral dead or dying, the rest of the marine life had followed suit.

When she'd first dived at this reef, back before her accident, before she'd even gone to Australia, it had been a vibrant landscape of marine life. Brightly coloured fish had swum in and out of the coral, and anemones had waved gently in the light current. She had known where to watch out for well-camouflaged stone fish, and where to give a wide berth to avoid getting too close to a lion fish. But global warming and other human interventions had worked fast, turning it into an underwater wasteland.

She tried not to despair. She was here; Guy was here. They were going to try to fix this. If she thought too much about what the reef had lost, she'd never be able to concentrate on what she needed to do to bring it back to life.

When she had all the pictures she needed she signed to Guy that they should head back to the boat, and then she bobbed up above the surface, checking that Guy was alongside her. She climbed back onto the deck of the boat, pulling off her mask and fins and squeezing salt water from her hair.

She was aware of Guy sitting next to her, taking off his equipment, but it wasn't until he spoke that she turned to look at him and saw the expression on his face.

'My God, what happened to it?' he asked, his face pale.

She narrowed her eyes.

'What do you mean?'

'I mean, the last time I saw it, it was teeming with life. We could barely move for fish.'

We? She didn't ask. Didn't want to know with whom he'd been here before.

'You've swum here before?' she asked, surprised that he'd not mentioned it yet.

He nodded. 'Last time I visited St Antoine.'

The shock was evident on his features, and she softened towards him a little. It was clear that he did care about the environment of the island, despite his impatience to move on the building project.

'What happened to it?' he asked again.

She explained about coral bleaching, the effects of rising sea temperatures and the impact of tourism and watched his face as the information sank in. She would have to wait and see whether that carried through to the decisions that he made as the project progressed. It was easy to be shocked by environmental issues when you were sitting on the water with the evidence right in front of you. In her experience, developers started caring a lot less about the coral when they were back in their offices, staring at a spreadsheet and a schedule.

Well, that was why she was here, she reminded herself—so that Guy wouldn't forget. She smirked to herself at the irony of the amnesiac being the one responsible for reminding someone of anything. She softened towards him, though. He clearly was very shocked by what he had seen.

'I know it's hard to see,' she said. She knew that all too well. It broke her heart, seeing what had become of what had once been a lively, vibrant reef. 'But this is why we're here. You're doing the right thing, putting this right before the building work starts. Not everyone would.'

Guy shook his head. 'Looks like we were too late.'

'Maybe not. I've seen other reefs recover.' Not many. Not often. But she had fresh young coral growing in the lab, waiting to be transplanted out. 'The situation's bad, but not hopeless,' she said as she steered them around the coral, back towards the little dock on Le Bijou. 'We have to try.'

* * *

Seven years hadn't seemed so long until he went down under the surface of the water and saw for himself the evidence of how much time had passed. How different the world was now compared to the last time that he had been here. How something that had once been beautiful had been so completely destroyed. Meena had said that maybe the reef could be saved, that they at least had to try. But he could see for himself that it was a lost cause.

When Meena had denied his applications for the permits he needed, he'd not been able to see it as anything but an inconvenience—and an expensive, time-consuming one at that. But now he could see why she was so concerned.

He looked around the island after he had waved her off in her boat and tried to imagine how it would look when the resort was finished. He had artists' renderings and a three-dimensional model, but they couldn't tell him how it would feel to lie on the beach with the resort behind him and the sea creeping towards his toes.

Could he lie on the sand, imagining what was happening to the crumbling coral below the sparkling water? That was why he was going to hire Meena, he reasoned. It would be her job to worry about that. Not his. And, now that he had seen her out here, he was satisfied that she knew what she was doing and he shouldn't have to worry about it any more.

Except, he owned this island now. He was always going to worry about it. He wondered, not for the first time, if he had made a mistake when he had bought it. He looked back at his thought-process; he'd been so sure that he was making a rational decision, but the more he pondered it the more he realised that he just couldn't bear the thought of anyone else having it.

He remembered the first time they had come to the island. Meena had mentioned it when they'd been sitting in the back of a different boat, on their way out to a group dive at the resort he'd visited before—back when he'd just finished university, had been an apprentice in the family's global, multi-million-dollar business, trying to impress his parents. Before he'd started his own company, trying to earn their respect if he couldn't have their love, instead being accused of trying to undercut them and steal corporate secrets. Long before he'd realised that it wouldn't matter how hard he tried: he would always be a disappointment to them.

That summer he'd noticed the beautiful dive instructor—of course he had. But, in a large group, he hadn't had a chance to speak to her. So, when he had spotted a space beside her on the boat, he'd jumped at the opportunity. They'd chatted as they'd motored through the waves out to the dive site. He'd not been able to take his eyes off her: the way her eyes had lit up with excitement as she'd explained the dive to him. The way she'd gestured with her hands to emphasise what she was saying. The passion in her voice as she'd spoken about the reef ecosystem.

They'd been diving at one of the larger reefs with the group, a regular stop on the tourist train. He'd wanted to see what was on offer at the other resorts on

St Antoine, still trying to find his place in the business for which he'd just found himself responsible decades before he'd expected it.

'If you want a quieter dive site,' she'd said, 'there's an island I love—Le Bijou.' 'The jewel'. 'I could take you out there some time, if you wanted.'

If he'd wanted? He was fairly sure that what he'd wanted had been written all over his face. He'd been too young, too green in business and too in love to have mastered hiding his feelings.

Anyway, back then, he'd had no reason to. He'd been free to fall for Meena. And he had—hard. And then he'd gone back to Australia and had waited for her to call. To email. To turn up on his doorstep as they had arranged. But she hadn't. He'd never heard a word from her.

Because she'd been lying in the clinic, with no idea who she was, never mind her feelings for anyone else.

And no one had called him about it, because no one had known about him. They had been so careful to keep their relationship a secret. She'd said that it was because he was a guest at the resort, the owner's son, and she just an employee. Because the conservative society of the island would judge their relationship. Would judge *her* for having a relationship with a white guy from a wealthy family.

She'd been worried that she would lose her job for breaking the rules. That the gossip that would follow her around the island would be unrelenting. He hadn't pushed her then because it hadn't occurred to him that he needed to. He'd gone back to Australia full of plans for their future, and when she hadn't turned up he'd assumed that she'd changed her mind about him. Her mobile number had stopped working. He couldn't ask about her at the resort without risking getting her into trouble. So he'd had to let it go.

Except he hadn't, had he? He'd buried his feelings in drink, had partied harder than he ever had before. Convinced himself that he was over Meena. He had started a relationship with a woman he'd met in a nightclub, who'd agreed that all he needed to cheer himself up was her and a bottle of something potent.

And it had worked, for a while. They'd distracted each other from the pain that had driven them to numb rather than face their feelings. Until the morning that he'd woken in a too-quiet flat to dozens of missed calls, and realised that something was horribly, horribly wrong.

And now it turned out that Meena hadn't abandoned him at all. The opposite. He was the one who had left her fighting life-threatening injuries. Alone. There could be no doubt that she was better off without him in her life. The sooner he could get off this island, get himself well away from her, the better.

She looked at him now and had no idea of what they had once shared. He'd come here because he'd wanted to wipe his memories of that time. To overwrite them. To overwrite the whole island. And instead he found himself as sole guardian of these memories—if he wanted the job. If he chose to forget, it would be as if they had never happened. But it didn't feel right, doing that. She had lost enough. He couldn't tell her what they had shared—not when being so close to him could bring her nothing but harm. Not when he himself knew that he couldn't offer what he had once promised.

Keeping it a secret was for the best. Telling her would only hurt her. It would have hurt him, if that was even possible any more. No. He had to plough on with the plans he had made before he had arrived here. Get work on the resort under way and then start forgetting he and Meena had ever been here. Even if it seemed that she was remotely interested in him. Which she most definitely didn't seem to be. He couldn't risk hurting her all over again. Even though he knew now that Meena hadn't meant to hurt him, that didn't change who it had made him.

The fact was that he hadn't been able to trust in any relationship that he'd had since then. His inability to trust and commit had hurt people. No—she was better off without him. Better off not knowing. If he told her how they had once felt about one another, she'd be curious. She'd have questions. She'd want to pick at wounds that had long ago scarred over.

He walked back towards his boat, feeling the sand beneath his feet, the sun pounding his shoulders. Was this it? The last time he would stand on their beach? The last chance to remember what they had shared here before he went back to Sydney, the bulldozers moved in and he moved on with his life?

CHAPTER FOUR

THIS WAS PROBABLY a huge mistake, Meena told herself for the hundredth time as she scrolled to Guy's office number on her phone and her thumb hovered over the call button. It was fine. She could just leave a message with Dev, letting him know that she was going to be visiting the site of one of her coral transplants. Let him know that Guy was welcome to join her if he was interested in how the restoration of the reef might go and then hang up. She wouldn't have to talk to Guy. And there was no way that he'd even turn up.

So why bother inviting him?

Because she wanted him to care, she told herself. When they had been on the boat before, she had seen the shock on his face at the state of the reef of Le Bijou. And at that moment she'd thought that maybe she'd misunderstood him. Yes, he wanted to build a big hotel complex on this beautiful, untouched island. But that didn't make him evil. He had offered to hire her to ensure that no harm—or, realistically, as little harm as possible—came to Le Bijou. That counted for something.

The look on his face when he'd seen the destruction of the reef haunted her. It was as if he had lost something important to him. She didn't want him to leave here thinking that the reef was a lost cause. That nothing they could do could restore it. She wasn't sure why it was so important to her, didn't want to look too closely at her motivations, but the fact remained that she was compelled to do something.

And it was time that she went to check on her other transplants anyway. They had been in the water for two years now and were growing better than anyone had hoped. Other sea life had returned to the area and a young, vibrant ecosystem was growing up again around the reef. She wanted Guy to see that. To understand that they didn't have to resign themselves to losing the reef by Le Bijou.

Was that the only reason? she asked herself. Or was the reality of the situation that she just wanted to see him again? That she had enjoyed spending time with him? Had enjoyed the sight of his bare chest, studying the shape of his calves, the blond hair on his arms.

She shook her head. She shouldn't be thinking that way about him. About anyone. Thinking that way about men had never led her anywhere good in the past.

So what if her body wanted him? She had been there before, she assumed, and listening to her body then had left her miscarrying alone, afraid of what would happen if her family or their friends ever found out what had happened. She had to be smarter than that.

She had to second-guess what she thought she wanted before her desires led her into any more trouble.

She didn't want to spend her life alone. And she assumed that at some point down the line maybe she'd meet a nice, sensible boy and have a nice, sensible marriage, just as she knew was expected of her. Her body had betrayed her in the past, her passions had left her hurt and alone, and she couldn't risk that happening again.

She chewed at her thumbnail as she listened to the phone ring. Maybe she'd get voicemail, she thought—hoped—and wouldn't even have to talk to Dev.

'Hello?'

The greeting in English threw her momentarily.

There was only one person who would answer the phone in English.

'Guy?' The last thing that she had expected was for him to answer his own phone. 'Where's Dev?'

'Meena?' She resisted a thrill at the thought that he had recognised her voice and forced down the sensation it had triggered in her belly.

'Guy, sorry, I wasn't expecting you.'

'You just called my office.'

'Yes, but…' But she'd been hoping she wouldn't have to speak to him? She knew how stupid that would sound and caught the words before they left her mouth.

She shook off her embarrassment and surprise and remembered that she was a professional. 'I'm diving at a reef today where we transplanted in some coral a couple of years ago. I wondered if you would like to see it. It'll give you an idea of what we might be able to achieve at Le Bijou with some careful conservation.'

She could imagine him in his office, looking at a packed schedule, amused that she thought that he could simply drop everything and head out to look at some coral. The silence at the other end of the line spoke volumes and she was about to die of embarrassment and hang up when he said, 'I can clear my day from four. Would that work?'

Clear his day? She'd been expecting another snatched hour at most. Hopefully by four the fierce lunchtime heat would have started to abate and being out on the water in her boat would be a little more bearable.

'That works for me,' she said, hoping that she was adequately hiding her surprise. 'Should I meet you there?'

'I'll pick you up,' he said. 'I prefer to dive from my own boat. Where shall I collect you?'

She hesitated, but then gave him the details of the marina, bristling at his overbearing tone. 'I'll see you in a few hours, then,' he said, sounding distracted, and then hung up.

The hours passed slowly, but as the clock ticked towards four she headed out to her boat to check and gather her diving equipment. Cursing herself for look-ing out over the water, she tried to catch sight of Guy's boat. She wasn't sure what to expect. The marinas around the island were peppered with super-yachts and speedboats more luxurious and expensive than she could possibly dream of owning. Judging by his taste in speedboats and snorkel equipment, she shouldn't expect Guy to have skimped.

She looked at the worn wooden boards and tired paintwork of her own vessel. She was proud of how she had kept it afloat all these years, having rescued and restored it when she'd been at university before she had gone to Australia. She wouldn't have made the strides she had in her education without it. It had allowed her to carry out the research that had won her a scholarship for her postgraduate study at the world-leading university in marine biology.

It had kick-started a career that had fallen by the wayside since her accident. After that had happened, she had needed to keep things simple. And sanding and oiling the board of this boat had brought her hours of pleasure. It had always been the plan to go back to Australia to work, to continue her research, which would have a far wider effect than saving a coral reef or two here on the islands. But after her accident she'd lost the drive to return. Had stayed home, and safe, instead.

A luxury yacht cruised into the marina and, though she could only see crew on board, she had no doubt that it was Guy's boat. It didn't have the company branding— it was clearly for pleasure, rather than business—but it had an unmistakable air of Guy Williams class.

She looked down at her humble, though no longer leaky, little boat. She couldn't summon any jealousy for the larger craft. Sure, luxury must be nice. She had heard, anyway. But she liked her own hands on the tiller, setting her own course. Liked being able to navigate around the coral and into the smallest lagoons.

She wouldn't swap the freedom of taking out her own boat alone, on her own whim, for the convenience of a couple of luxury cabins and a well-stocked bar. Well, not for more than an afternoon or so, anyway.

She watched the yacht slow to a standstill, and then launch a speedboat from the aft deck. Of course. She smiled. Of course.

As Guy drew closer she waved from her own mooring and saw the change in his posture when he spotted her. Creasing her eyes against the glare of the sun, she wished she could read him better. She sensed there was more to him than just the brusque businessman he presented to the world. Certainly, in her dreams there was a lot more to him.

It was just fantasy, she reminded herself. However real those dreams felt. However often she was having them—and she was having them a lot—they weren't real. She didn't know him better because she had dreamed of his hands on her body and his whispers in her hair. And she would do very well to remember that.

He tied his boat to the dock, jumped up onto the worn wooden planks of the walkway and headed over to her.

She straightened her shoulders, resisting the urge to lift a hand to her hair, which was being caught and played by the ocean breeze, the only respite against the heat of the summer day.

'Guy.' She pasted on a neutral smile. 'Hi. I'm glad you could make it.'

He nodded. 'Yes,' he said. That one syllable was

maddeningly vague. Yes, he was glad he was here too? Yes, he knew she was glad he was here? She was starting to see that Guy Williams was pretty opaque, impossible to read, even without her amnesia in the mix making her second-guess every man that she met, looking for clues to a shared past.

'Good,' Meena said, attempting to be equally enigmatic. 'Let me just grab my gear and we can head off.' She started lugging air tanks and the bags containing her dive gear from the small cabin, but froze at the feel of Guy's hand on her shoulder.

It shouldn't do that to her, she reasoned. It shouldn't make her stop like that, as if the rest of the world had ceased to matter and there was just him, her and touch. She should be able to breathe normally, even when he was standing so close. Her skin should feel like just skin, rather than a tissue-thin, failing barrier between her and pure sensation, fireworks, lightning strikes and every cliché she could think of, all from the innocent touch of a hand on a shoulder. She was starting to see, being around Guy, how she must have got it so wrong last time. How easily her body could be led astray by a man she desired, whoever that man in her past had been. How he had made her forget what was important to her.

Well, this time, she was prepared. She knew the consequences of oohing and aahing over those fireworks. Of looking to find where those sensations led. She wasn't going to make the mistake with Guy that she had made in the past. He was leaving the island in two weeks anyway. As if she needed another reason why she couldn't act on her feelings.

At least she didn't have to try to convince herself that following these feelings she had for Guy would be an equally colossal mistake. She was well aware of the fact. Every rational, sensible part of her brain—at least, all of those that she could readily access—was signalling to her on high alert that he was dangerous. Dangerous to the status quo. To her way of moving through the world, which was largely based on avoiding entanglements with the opposite sex.

'You can leave it, if you want,' Guy said. 'I have some on the yacht you can borrow.'

If she hadn't already seen his snorkelling equipment, she might have hesitated. But she knew that his scuba gear would be top of the range too. If you were stocking a luxury yacht for a dive, you were hardly going to cut corners. And if it would save her having to lift and carry her air tanks, she would say yes to anything. She threw her dive watch, underwater camera and dive plan into her backpack, though—those were non-negotiable—and accepted Guy's offer.

'Okay, sure, thanks,' she said, locking the strong box and stepping up on to the walkway.

'So what's the plan?' Guy asked as they jumped down onto his speedboat and left the sleepy Saturday afternoon capital behind them.

'Deeper water,' Meena said with a smile. 'There's a few reefs on the ocean side of the island that have coped better than most over the last few years. We collected coral fragments from them after a storm and grew them out in the lab. Then we transplanted them on to the reefs that were suffering the worst from bleaching. We're checking them both out today.'

'Does it harm the healthy reef, taking the fragments?' Guy asked.

Meena pulled a face. 'It's not a perfect solution, because those fragments would normally fall and grow on the reefs nearby. But I don't want to go breaking handfuls of coral off a healthy reef. So...it's the best we have. It's a risk. And if it doesn't take on the other reef—it's heartbreaking,' she admitted.

A huge part of her job was weighing up benefits and risks like this, and it felt as though the stakes couldn't be higher. And so much of the time it didn't work. The damage that had been done was irreversible.

'But sometimes, like the reef we're going to see today, the transplant takes, the coral grows, the fish and all the other marine life come back and it's...' She smiled and gestured with her hands as she searched for the right word. 'It's...*glorieux*,' she said at last. *It's glorious.*

She was glorious, Guy thought as the gentle breeze off the water teased her hair into soft tangles and her passion for the reef brought a glow to her face that he recognised from a younger Meena. She invested so much in these reefs. It was obvious from the look on her face when she spoke about them how personally she took each success and failure.

Had that been there before? he asked himself, trying to remember. Back then, he was pretty sure that he'd been only interested in her passion for *him*. That wasn't fair, he corrected himself. It hadn't just been about lust, or the thrill of the chase. It hadn't been a physical thing. Or *just* a physical thing. Though, while they were talking about glorious...

The connection between them had gone deeper than that. They'd cared for one another. Cared for one another's passions as well. It seemed important to him now that he was the only keeper of those memories that he got them right.

He'd come here wanting to forget, to pour concrete over his memories. To stop them seeping into his consciousness, making it impossible to move on. But once he'd found out about her amnesia that hadn't seemed fair any more. He couldn't tell her about what had happened between them that summer. Not without hurting her. But if he wiped those memories from his own mind too then they were truly gone. He was the backup copy. And Meena had lost so much already that he didn't want to take that from her as well.

After they had swum together alone the other day, he had known that spending more time together— just the two of them—was a bad idea, but here they were. It would be too easy to slip back into old ways of thinking. Old ways of feeling. He had to remember that things were different now. That *he* was different now. That the things that he'd had to offer her back then were no longer his to give. He had wanted to love her. To protect her. To be her partner. But he'd failed her back then, and failed the woman he had replaced her with, and he knew that it would happen again. And he wouldn't hurt her like that again. She had spent seven years moving on from what they had shared, and lost, and he wouldn't drag her back.

'What do you hope to see?' he asked, keeping their focus on the dive.

'I want to check the transplant sites first; make sure that the new coral is still growing well. We used a couple of different attachment methods, so it'll be interesting to see whether there's any difference in how they are faring. I'll need to survey the marine life, as well, to see if there are any new arrivals since I checked it last month.'

He nodded; that all seemed reasonable. 'I'll show you to where you can get changed,' Guy said as they both looked up to the full height of the yacht. The little speedboat had brought them to the lower deck and the white of the cabin towered, blindingly bright, above them.

He could let a steward show her to the guest cabin that he'd put aside for her use. That would be the sensible thing to do. But it was inhospitable, he justified to himself. She was his guest on the yacht, so it was his responsibility as host to make sure she was comfortable.

That was a lie. He wanted to spend time with her. He was excited by her presence in his life and he wanted to make the most of it. There was no point denying the way that he was drawn to her. But that didn't mean that he was going to be stupid about it. He knew that he was bad news for her. Knew that he was walking on glass, trying to keep their shared history from her even if he genuinely believed that knowing the truth could only hurt her.

As they climbed the steps to the upper deck of the yacht, he wondered what she would make of it. The Meena that he had known so many years ago wouldn't have been impressed by it. She loved the boat that she had rescued from a junk yard before university and had lovingly restored. He had felt a pang in his gut when he had seen it earlier, remembering all the times they had taken that boat out to Le Bijou. It had been their escape, somewhere they could relax without the fear of being spotted by someone from the resort, without risking Meena's job.

He watched her as they moved along the yacht. Her eyes had widened as they had entered the main cabin, but he could see the slight rise of her eyebrows that showed that she was amused rather than impressed by the luxury.

He had bought this yacht, as he had done almost everything else in the last few years, because it was the furthest thing that he could imagine from how they'd travelled around the islands when he had been on St Antoine before. He hadn't wanted to remember her boat. Hadn't been able to think about going out on it with her. That was why he had taken the speed-boat to meet her on Le Bijou. It was only when he'd seen that she had that unfamiliar glass-bottomed boat that he had finally decided that he would go out on the water with her.

They arrived at the cabin and he hesitated at the door. Crossing the threshold of her private cabin was a line both literal and metaphorical that he wasn't prepared to cross.

'You can change in here,' he told her. 'The stewards will get you anything you need.'

He turned to go, but the sound of Meena's voice pulled him back.

'This yacht is very impressive, Guy.'

Of course it was. It was all part of the image. He owned a string of luxury resorts. His billionaire customers expected to see the owner playing the part. More important, they expected to be wined and dined by him occasionally, and the yacht was a part of the deal. It was all for show. So why did it bother him that she saw that? That she saw through the image that he had constructed?

Why did that ironic crook of her eyebrow unsettle him?

'I'll meet you on the lower deck. The equipment is all down there, but there are wetsuits in the wardrobe here. Choose whichever you prefer.' He turned away so that she couldn't read his face. He hadn't expected her still to be able to read him. He'd assumed that that had been lost along with her memories. But he had the uncomfortable feeling that there was still something there, some understanding of who he was.

He headed to his own cabin and changed into his swim shorts before he headed down to the deck where the dive gear was kept to change into his wetsuit and wait for Meena to arrive. As he pulled the neoprene over his legs, working the tight fabric up his body, he steeled himself for the sight of Meena in hers. He had seen her in a rash suit just a few days ago and, though he had averted his eyes as much as possible, the sight of her body in that skintight material had brought back more memories than he could comfortably handle.

He heard bare feet padding up behind him and turned to see Meena walking along the side deck towards him. It was good that he had prepared himself because, even with trying to keep his eyes locked somewhere over her shoulder, his peripheral vision couldn't miss the fact that the wetsuit emphasised the sumptuous curves of breasts, waist and hips.

Once, his hands had known those curves as well as they had known his own body. Over the course of that summer, they had explored her body together until he hadn't known where he had ended and she'd begun. He would lie with her in his arms, her limbs entwined with his, feeling the rise and fall of her breath as if it had been his own.

As one of the stewards showed Meena where the various masks, fins, air tanks and other equipment were stored, Guy kept his gaze fixed firmly out on the water, aware that he was being rude. But that was infinitely better than the alternative, which was turning to look and talk to her, knowing that he wouldn't be able to keep his feelings under control. He couldn't allow that to happen.

He pulled on fins and his gas tanks, feeling their protection like a charm. It was impossible to find someone anything other than funny in full scuba equipment, and he was counting on that to see them through today. He concentrated on the dive plan as she talked him through it, impressed by her attention to detail. Though he had no reason to be surprised. She had taught him to dive, after all. He knew how good she was. He checked his watch and with a final nod at Meena tipped himself backwards from the side of the boat.

As the water engulfed him, he took a second to orient himself in the whiteout of bubbles and then surfaced to look and see that Meena had followed him into the water.

He gave her the okay sign as the water settled around her as the ocean adjusted to their presence.

The reef started just a few metres away, and he put his face under the water, marvelling as he always did at that line between the above and the below—the reflective mirror of the surface that hid the wealth of life underneath the surface. As he watched, schools of neon fish darted past in flashes of yellow and blue, and as he relaxed below the surface, his breaths slowing into the familiar huff of the regulator, he began to take in more—anemones swishing in the current, the slow crawl of a hermit crab down on the sand.

He looked over at Meena, who signed that they should dive deeper, and he gave her another okay sign. It was a long time since he'd dived, and he'd forgotten the otherworldly feeling of being beneath the water, his soundscape reduced to the slow, steady rhythms of his own breath and heartbeat, light restricted to those rays that struggled through the body of the ocean, growing fewer and dimmer the deeper that they dived.

He followed Meena's fins through the water, looking when she turned and pointed out something on the reef that he hadn't noticed. A tiny crab, a sea snake, a lion fish guarding its territory, spines erect and fearsome. They skirted away from that last one, giving it plenty of room, not wanting the underwater emergency of a nasty sting even through the neoprene of their wetsuits.

The yacht was a dark shadow on the surface of the water, growing more distant as they rounded another side of the reef. Meena stopped again and pointed her index and middle fingers in a V at her mask, divers' sign language for 'look', and then pointed into a dark nook of the reef. He didn't want to risk damaging the coral with his fins by getting too close, so he stayed as still as he could, calling to mind everything he had learned about buoyancy in order to be completely immobile above the reef. Mask below fins, breathing slowly and steadily, he didn't even need to adjust his buoyancy control to keep him in position.

He followed where Meena was pointing to what seemed like a stony piece of coral. But as he watched longer, buffeted only slightly by a gentle current, he realised that he was looking at a stone fish. Something he never would have noticed if he hadn't been with Meena. Something he would have swum straight past if he hadn't been with someone who knew these reefs like they were a part of her. He looked up, the regulator in his mouth making it impossible to smile, but from the expression on Meena's face his excitement must have been showing in his eyes.

He slowly swam up from the reef until he could

gently kick his fins without risking touching the coral. As they continued on around the reef, Meena taking photos and pointing out where new pieces of coral had been cemented or tied into place, he lost count of the number of species that he saw. The contrast with the reef at Le Bijou, where they had snorkelled together, was astonishing. And he knew that he would do anything that he could to restore the reefs there. Seeing that it could be done, that it had been done here, was more moving than he could have expected.

Through perseverance, stubbornness and her meticulous research, Meena had found a way to turn the clock back here. To undo the damage wreaked by careless tourists and the inexorable warming of the seas; to bring life back to this barren reef. He could have watched it all day. Watched the fish darting and the anemones swaying, and Meena click, click, clicking away with her camera. Always looking for more information, more ideas, more ways to help return this ecosystem to its former glory.

When she was finished with her camera she glanced at her watch and then with a thumbs-up sign suggested that they return to the surface. He signalled okay and kicked his fins as they swam straight up. They hadn't dived deep enough to need more than a quick safety stop, so they kicked up through the water, his fins an extension of his body propelling him gently, as if he were a creature of the ocean rather than the interloper that his gas tanks and wetsuit proved him to be.

As they broke the surface, Guy looked over to make sure Meena was still with him. They had surfaced away from the yacht but he knew that his crew would be watching for him. Would bring the speedboat over to collect them if he gave them the signal. But the sea life beneath them was so tranquil, so delicately balanced with the new coral transplants and the recently returned marine life, that he didn't want to disrupt it by bringing the boat closer and scaring away the fish.

Or maybe it was that he didn't want to disrupt this, he thought as Meena pulled off her mask and smiled at him. Under the water, there had been no place for complications. No thoughts about their past, or what they had been to each other before. Diving together, they were responsible for keeping one another safe. It was important to be in the moment. To communicate. There were enough barriers between them, with not being able to speak to each other beyond simple hand signals, to prevent anything to distract them.

But now that they were back above the surface, back in the real world, those doubts came flooding back. He never should have mentioned that they had known each other before. He had seen how she had reacted to that. How she had started to wonder whether she had the full story. Had tried slotting that new piece of information into her memories and seeing if it stirred up anything else.

He was suddenly struck with doubt that he was doing the right thing by keeping their past from her. But he couldn't see a way of telling her without hurting her. He had loved her then, and she him, but he didn't—couldn't—love her any more.

What if she had questions? How could he tell her

what he had done, who he had become? No. He had been right the first time round. Telling Meena could only lead to more pain for them both. Knowing what they had shared, what they had lost, felt like a knife in his chest every time that he saw her. Every time he remembered what they had hoped for in their relationship, and how pitiful the reality had turned out to be. He couldn't spare himself that pain but he could spare her. And he would. He owed her that.

They swam over to the boat with barely a word spoken, just a smile passing between them. With his buoyancy adjusted, it felt more like floating, a lazy kick of his fins moving him through the water with barely any effort. They climbed aboard the yacht, water dripping from their wetsuits puddling around their feet on the smooth, oiled deck, as his staff appeared to collect their dive gear and hand out warm, fluffy towels and dressing gowns.

With the activity around them, he could barely see Meena. He glanced over her way to say something, but when he saw her hand on the zip at the back of her suit he immediately looked away. He didn't want to see that. Never mind that it wasn't appropriate to watch her as she was undressing. He couldn't. To be reminded of the wonder of her body would be too much. The reminder of making love to her. Of how she had trusted him. And he her. How together they had explored one another, fulfilled one another. Loved one another.

He pulled on a towelling robe over his tight, wet

swim shorts and waited until Meena cleared her throat before looking round again.

'That was wonderful,' she said, her expression matching the smile and passion in her words. 'The coral is doing even better than the last time that I was here.'

Guy couldn't help but return her smile. 'Shall we dry off,' he suggested, 'and have a drink while we talk about it?'

'Perfect. I have so many ideas for Le Bijou. I'd like to know what you think of them.'

She'd been so inspired by what she had seen on the reef, she couldn't wait to adjust her plans for how to put that into action. Her mind raced with ideas as she headed back to the cabin to change.

When she emerged, clean and dry in a cotton sun-dress, the sun was lower in the sky, its burning intensity now merely a hot glow on her skin. Still, she pulled her shades over her eyes, as glad for the subtle barrier they would provide between her and Guy as she was for their UV protection. But when she reached the deck Guy was nowhere to be seen. A steward had left a selection of drinks in an ice bucket, and a basket overflowing with fruit on a table between two sun loungers stretched under a sun shade, so she poured herself a glass of water and perched on the edge of one of the loungers, waiting for Guy to appear.

He strode out onto the deck with the confidence only a man on his own yacht possessed and came to sit beside her. Grabbing a beer from the ice bucket, he flipped off the lid and sat back.

'So what was your verdict on the coral?' he asked, looking across at her as he eased back onto the lounger. 'Were you happy with how it was doing?'

She could feel herself glow with pleasure as she answered him. 'I really was. There's such a difference from the last time that I was here.' So many of the bare, dead areas of coral were now teeming with life, and she'd recorded at least a dozen species that had moved in since her last survey. She couldn't have hoped for a better result. 'What did you think of it?' she asked.

He smiled, and she was tempted to melt at the way the lines softened his face. It made him more human. 'It was a relief, to be honest, after seeing the reef by Le Bijou. That was how I remember the diving here. Was it as bad as Le Bijou?' Guy asked. 'Before the transplant, I mean.'

She noticed that mention of diving here before, and again it tugged at something in her mind. A memory lurking just out of reach. She shook the feeling off, trying to stay in the present. Resisting the pull to that black hole in her memories.

'It was different,' she said. 'Not exactly as bad, but it definitely wasn't good. We've made a real difference. We have every reason to hope that we can replicate the results.'

Guy's smile took her aback.

'Well, anyone would think you actually care,' Meena said, smiling back at him.

He frowned. 'Of course I care, Meena. Why do you think I came?'

Of course he had come because he wanted to see the coral, she chided herself. Did he think that she was sitting here imagining that he had some sort of ulterior motive for seeing her? She could laugh at that. *Should* laugh at that. The only answer that made sense was that he had a real interest in how the reef was recovering. How that could be applied to Le Bijou.

So that he could get his building permits.

As her brain raced through the permutations of the different reasons that Guy could have had to come out to the dive today, of course it all came back to that. He wanted his permits so that he could get his building project moving again and get off the island.

'I'm sorry. I shouldn't have said that. I know that you care,' Meena said quickly.

'You should know,' Guy said, and then stiffened, as if he had said something wrong. Meena watched, confused, as his body language became more and more uncomfortable. Eventually, he sat up on the edge of the lounger, facing her, his expression deadly serious.

'What do you mean by that?' she asked, the tension in his body contagious, putting her on edge too. They were sitting so close their knees were almost touching, their pose laughably tense on two pieces of furniture designed specifically for relaxation.

'Nothing,' he said, refusing to meet her eye.

'It's not nothing,' she countered, trusting her gut. Trusting that feeling that there was a memory lurking just a little way out of reach. Trusting that Guy was hiding something, something that she would want to know.

'Why should I know that you care?' Meena asked. 'I've only known you a week. You've not wowed me with your passion for environmental conservation. There's something you're not telling me. What is it?'

She stared him down. She needed him to be truthful with her. She had spent so long questioning her body. Questioning her mind. Now she just knew that she was right about this. She had picked up on something that Guy had said and now she needed him to follow through and fill in the blanks.

'It's nothing,' Guy said.

'You're lying.' She held his gaze a little longer. 'Why?'

He shifted uncomfortably on the lounger, then stood and walked over to the railing, turning his back on her and looking out over the ocean.

'I'm right, aren't I?' Meena asked, watching his back. 'You're hiding something from me.'

'I'm trying to do the right thing here,' he said, turning around and leaning back against the rail, his arms crossed over his body.

'Let me make that easy for you,' she said, walking over to him, feeling perspiration prickle her skin in the late afternoon sun as she mirrored his crossed arms, holding his gaze and refusing to back down. 'Tell me the truth.'

'I don't want to hurt you, Meena.'

There was something in the familiar tone of his voice, the way that his eyes softened as he looked at her, that told her most of what she needed to know. They weren't strangers. Hadn't been strangers even when she'd met him on the beach a week ago. He had known her before. Remembered her from when he had stayed at his parents' resort on St Antoine seven years ago, before her accident.

That hole in her memory loomed before her, menacing with its secrets and the hidden parts of her soul. He knew what lurked in there; she was sure of it. And, if she wanted to know, she was sure that she could make him tell her.

Was it him? Was he the mystery man she had been looking for all this time? And, if he was, did she want to know for sure?

She knew she could find out now if she pushed. He would tell her.

But she didn't know if she was ready.

'I don't want you to hurt me either,' she told him.

Guy shook his head, arms dropping from where they had been crossed to grip the railing behind him. 'Then don't make me talk about that time.'

She thought for a few long seconds about letting this lie. About protecting herself from whatever it was that he thought would hurt her. She could leave this yacht and they could never mention this conversation again. When Guy was gone from the island, she would never have to think about him again.

But the unease in her chest as she considered it told her what she needed to know—she had to find out what had happened to her that summer. Who she had become. She had spent the last seven years of her life wondering about that time. She couldn't turn away from this opportunity, even if it did mean more pain. What could be worse than not knowing who she had been? Who she was now?

'I need to know, Guy. I need you to tell me everything.'

He let out a long sigh, lifted a hand and rubbed at his hair, and a chill went down Meena's spine at the expression on his face. If they had been romantically involved before, if he was the man that she'd lost her virginity to, then she would expect embarrassment. Not fear. Not this pain that etched lines into his forehead.

'I've already guessed that we knew each other that summer,' she said. 'But my memories are missing,' she added, hoping that would prompt him to continue. 'How did we meet?'

The look on his face had already confirmed what she had been starting to suspect. That he was her mystery boyfriend from that summer. But his expression was scaring her, rather than reassuring her. What had happened between them to cause the pain that was so clearly emanating from him?

'We were friends, weren't we? More than friends.' She made it a statement, rather than a question.

She couldn't tell him how she knew, though. Couldn't tell him she'd known all along that she'd had a lover that summer because she'd been pregnant. Unless he already knew that. She'd been six weeks along when the accident had happened. Had she told him? Had she even known herself? This was why she needed to know.

Guy shook his head, and for a moment she thought that he was going to deny everything. If he did that, she wouldn't know what to do next. She would know that he was lying. His face had already told her that they had a past. What she needed now were the details.

'Yes, we knew each other,' Guy said without meeting her eyes.

'More than knew each other. We were…involved.'

He looked up then, meeting her gaze briefly before looking away again. 'Yes. We were involved.'

CHAPTER FIVE

INVOLVED. THAT ONE word didn't come anywhere near to what they had been to each other. He had never even wanted to reveal this much. But she'd looked at his face and read exactly what she needed to know. He'd expected her to have lost that knack. They barely knew each other any more. She shouldn't be able to see into his thoughts like that. But, as usual, he had underestimated her.

So what if she knew that they had been involved, though? Could that be enough for her? Could he extricate himself from this conversation without having to open a vein and bleed every single moment of their history onto the deck in front of her?

'We had sex?' she asked, doing away with euphemisms.

His head snapped up at the question and he held her gaze. Her expression was fierce, and he knew that he couldn't lie to her.

'Yes, we had sex.'

It seemed both so simple and so cold to say those four words. They didn't come anywhere close to describing what they had shared. But revealing even that much was going much further than he had ever wanted.

What was he meant to say? *Yes, we had sex. I loved you, but you never came to me. You broke my heart, and me. And now I'm dangerous and no good for you and I'm not going to risk hurting you by telling you all this.*

But of course he couldn't.

Knowing now that it wasn't her fault that she had never come to Australia didn't matter. He didn't hold that against her, wasn't angry. How could he possibly be, in the circumstances? But, even though it hadn't been intentional, the damage had still been done. He had made the decisions that he had made, and someone had died. He couldn't undo that. Would never be free of the responsibility or the guilt. The wound to his heart had turned him into someone who hurt the people he tried to love.

If only he had been there. If he had managed to curb his drinking enough to actually make it out of his apartment and to the nightclub, he could have stopped his girlfriend, Charlotte, taking those pills. He would have noticed that she needed help. He would have called an ambulance before she collapsed and everything would have been different. She would have been alive and he wouldn't have been a monster. But that hadn't happened. Instead he had downed beer after beer and then a bottle of whisky, trying to drown his memories and numb himself enough to get out of the house and face the people he called his friends.

He wasn't making that mistake again.

After Charlotte had died he'd stopped the partying. Stopped the drinking. Had concentrated on growing his business. But he could never forget what had happened. And he had no doubt in his mind that if he and Meena started a relationship again one of them, or both of them, would get very badly hurt, and he had no interest in either outcome.

Guy tried to read the expression on Meena's face as she took in what he had said. The shock at his straight answer came first; that one was clear. But it mellowed into something subtler. Something he was less sure of.

'Just once?' she asked eventually.

He huffed in a deep breath. He could lie. But he'd had enough of lying. He would answer her questions truthfully. But that didn't mean he had to volunteer anything more than she asked for.

'No. More than once.'

'But then you left.' She narrowed her eyes at him, taking a step closer. He could feel her scrutiny on his face. In his heart.

'Yes.'

'Why?' Her arms remained crossed, her expression unreadable now. Not quite hurt. Not quite curious. Somewhere between the two, perhaps.

'Because the summer was over.'

He caught the huff and the eye roll that let him know she didn't believe him. It wasn't the whole truth. But it wasn't a lie. 'And you never knew about my accident?'

'No,' he said softly. 'I swear I never did. Not until

you told me yourself.' It was important that she believed him on that. Whatever else had happened between them, he didn't want her to think he was the sort of man who would have left her to cope with that alone, not if he had known what she'd been going through.

'And why did you decide not to tell me about all this?' This question was forced out through gritted teeth, and he understood for the first time what a risk he had taken by keeping the truth from her until now. He had to make Meena see that he had only ever acted in what he'd thought were her best interests, even if it didn't seem that way now. He had only ever wanted to save her from the hurt that he felt every time he remembered what they had once been to each other. But, again, that was more than Meena needed to know. He wasn't lying to her any longer.

'It didn't seem relevant…any more.'

'It didn't seem relevant to our current working relationship that we used to have sex with each other?'

He shook his head, firm in his resolve to protect himself. To protect Meena. He would give her the facts that she needed to fill in the blanks in her memories. But she had no claim on knowing his emotions. Those were his and his alone.

'No,' he said bluntly.

Unforgivably bluntly.

'Why not?' she asked, clearly determined not to let him off the hook so easily.

'Because it's in the past.' He uncrossed his arms and rubbed his hands through his hair, wondering how long this Q&A was going to last. The longer it went on, the harder it was to conceal what his feelings for her had once been. And if that came out then, yes, this would get complicated. 'I thought if you couldn't remember it, it was less complicated not to tell you,' he said with complete honesty.

'So you lied to me.' Her brow creased together in a way that made him uncomfortably aware that she was not going to take his answers at face value. Of course she wasn't. When had she ever? She was too smart not to have figured this out. Not to keep probing at his feelings until he had revealed everything. But he was on his guard, and he wasn't going to let her do that. 'Even though I told you how hard it was, living with these holes in my memory.'

'I tried not to lie,' Guy said.

Though in truth he hadn't really tried that hard. He should have told her sooner. He saw that now. But he had been trying to protect her. He winced a bit at that thought. That wasn't entirely honest, he acknowledged. She wasn't the only one he was trying to protect.

'You failed,' she stated.

He nodded. 'And I'm sorry for that. There won't be any more lies.'

She held his gaze but didn't answer for a long time.

'I still don't remember.'

His face softened with sympathy. How could it not, in the face of what she had suffered, and the disappointment in her voice? 'Did you think...?'

'That my memories would be back in a flood? No, not really,' she admitted, looking downcast. 'But I'd hoped that maybe there'd be...something.'

His arms ached to pull her in at seeing the despondency in her expression. He fought it, hard, and spoke instead. 'You said you knew that we were together before. How did you know that?'

She shrugged, blushing a little. 'You were behaving strangely. I just guessed the reason.' She looked away, though, which made him think that this time she was the one keeping secrets.

Fine, she could keep them if she wanted. The less they said about the past, the better, as far as he was concerned. He had meant what he'd said. What had happened in the past made no difference to who they were now. They had a business relationship and nothing more. All he needed was to get these permits signed off and get off this island. Then Meena could continue working with the project manager and he would never have to speak to her again.

A pang of regret hit him in the chest with that thought.

It was just an echo, he told himself. An echo of the feelings that he used to have for her. That wasn't what he felt now. It would be a relief, he told himself, to be off St Antoine and away from Meena. Except that thought didn't seem to ease his pain.

It was him, Meena told herself with certainty. She'd known deep down as soon as she'd seen that expression on his face that he was the one. By the time she'd asked the question, she already had the answer.

And yet, she didn't have the answer. She had a thousand more anxieties and a thousand more unresolved questions.

But this she knew: she had had sex with Guy Williams. More than once. And from the blank, expressionless look on Guy's face, it had meant less than nothing to him. So why had she done it? How could he sit with her, talk with her and dive with her now as if nothing had ever happened?

Why hadn't he known about the accident? Why had he never got in touch?

Now it was answered, what had seemed like the most important question in her life seemed suddenly irrelevant. She'd had sex—that wasn't new information. She'd known it since she'd been in the clinic.

But all along she'd thought that knowing the 'who' would answer all the other questions that she had. Principal amongst them: why? Why had she changed her mind about waiting? She knew that Guy was attractive. Knew that her body reacted whenever she saw him. That she wanted him. She'd thought that as soon as she knew who her partner had been, who had fathered the baby that she had been carrying, everything else would make sense. Her life, her decisions.

She'd been wrong.

Because nothing that she knew about Guy Williams made her decisions any more understandable. He was cold. He was evasive. He was bulldozing her island, or as good as.

How could this man have been the one? How could she ever possibly know? It wasn't as if she could ask him outright. It was clear in every line of his body and his face that he didn't want to talk about their past. He had said he wouldn't tell her any more lies, but how was she meant to get the important questions out: did you love me? Did I love you? Did you know that we were going to have a baby? Would you have been happy? Why did I love you? *Who was I when we were together?*

She couldn't even think about posing a single one of those questions to the hard, stern man standing in front of her, answering her questions with monosyllables while the breeze whipped at his hair.

There had been a moment when they were diving, communicating using only their eyes and their hands, when she had thought that she had felt a connection between them. An understanding and a shorthand that spoke of some deeper understanding than the one that they had formed over the last week. That was what had given her the confidence to ask the question that needed to be asked.

But it turned out that she had been wrong. Sex didn't equal intimacy. Or, if it ever had, it didn't apply indefinitely. The knowledge that Guy had once been inside her body didn't mean that she knew him any better now. And it didn't mean that she understood herself better, either.

What had she expected? She wasn't sure, but she did know what she'd wanted. She'd wanted to meet the man that she had fallen for, and she'd wanted every decision she'd made in the past, whether she could remember it or not, suddenly to make sense. She wanted to lose this shame and doubt that had dogged her since she had woken from her accident in a broken body with a broken mind and a broken heart.

But she'd been foolish, childish, thinking that that was going to be the outcome. All she knew now was what she'd known before. She'd had sex with a man who no longer wanted to be a part of her life.

Now that she knew that for certain, it was time to move on. To put to rest the questions that had been burning through her. To concentrate on the future, rather than focussing her energies on something that couldn't be changed. And that meant moving on from Guy. The more distance she could put between them, the better.

CHAPTER SIX

GUY GLANCED AT the inbox that he shared with his assistant, hoping for a message from Meena. Because he needed these permits sorted so he could get home to Sydney, he told himself. Not because he was feeling awkward over their last conversation, when he had confessed that they had been lovers and that he had returned to Australia and never been in touch again.

But three days had passed since she had made her excuses and they had awkwardly parted at the marina and there had been no word from her since. He wasn't surprised that she didn't want to rehash that last conversation, but he had been expecting to hear something about the report from their last dive. Without a plan for the reef at Le Bijou, she wouldn't sign off the permits. He wanted off this island, and he needed Meena's co-operation if that was going to happen.

He drew in a pained breath and reached for his phone, scrolling through his contacts until he found her number. As he listened to the ringing tone, he dropped his head into his hand, sure that this was a bad idea. If he was thinking as a developer, this call was essential. As her ex, it was a disaster waiting to happen; he was certain of it. But if she was avoiding him because of their last conversation, and that was holding up the development, then he needed to address the situation.

Just as he was about to hang up and send an email instead, the ringing stopped.

'Hello,' Meena said, a little out of breath. 'Sorry, I was in the lab,' she added by way of explanation for the delay.

Guy gulped, suddenly lost for words. 'We need to talk,' he said eventually.

'Guy, I...' He could hear the hesitation in Meena's voice and it actually reassured him. Hopefully she was as disinclined as he was to rehash their past.

'We need to talk about Le Bijou,' he added resolutely, leaving no room for her to interpret his last comment as being about their personal rather than professional life. 'I want to know what progress you have made since the dive.'

Meena took a deep breath to reply, but on an impulse he cut off whatever she was about to say.

'It would be best if you came here,' Guy said. 'I want this sorted as soon as possible. The best way to do that is in person. That way we can be sure there are no more delays.' He glanced at the clock in the corner of his computer screen. 'This afternoon?'

Meena paused, and he was already preparing to counter her arguments when she said, 'Fine. I'll be there in an hour. But I'll need to finish before sunset.'

'Sunset?' he asked, momentarily confused.

'I'm watching for turtles hatching on the beach tonight,' she explained. 'I'm not signing off the permits until I know what's going on with the nesting site. It's the last possible day of the incubation period, and I want to be there in person to see what's happening.'

'Fine,' he said. 'I'll see you in an hour.'

He watched the minutes crawl by slowly for the next sixty-four, and was about to pick up his phone and find out where Meena was when a knock sounded at the door. He looked up to see her standing in the doorway, laptop case slung over her shoulder, a hard look on her face.

'Where are we going to do this?' she asked without preamble.

He wasn't sure what he had been expecting from her today. But he was sure that it wasn't this…hardness in her eyes and her body. If she cared at all that they had once been lovers, she wasn't letting it show now.

He gestured her over to the table, then pulled out a couple of chairs for them both. 'Have you written your report on the dive?' he asked while she was booting up her computer.

She nodded, not looking over at him. 'It's nearly done,' she said, still looking at her blank screen.

How were they meant to work together if she couldn't even look at him? He understood that this was awkward. God, of course it was. But this was about more than their personal relationship. His whole development was dependent on getting these permits approved. If she couldn't even talk to him, they weren't going to get anywhere.

He hadn't exactly helped matters, he acknowledged.

Now that she was in his office, it suddenly seemed like an insane idea. They could have done this over email. Over the phone. There were a million ways to finish this project without ever being in the same room, never mind holed up in his office together. And he hadn't thought that any of them were good enough. He had insisted that she come here, and had made them both uncomfortable.

'Meena?' he asked, trying to keep the frustration out of his voice.

'What?' she asked, not looking up.

'Will you look at me?' he asked.

She shrugged, finally looking over and meeting his eye. 'I am.'

'You know what I mean.'

She shook her head. 'I really don't, Guy. What's the problem?'

She was putting on a front. He could see that. He had thought that he remembered everything there was to know about her when he had seen her lying on the beach on Le Bijou nearly two weeks ago. But the more time that they had spent together, more was coming back to him. The easier it was to know what she was thinking from the set of her mouth or the angle of one dark, angled eyebrow.

'You're stalling,' he said, calling her bluff. 'That's the problem. This report should have been done days ago.'

She crossed her arms, leaning back in her chair, aiming a death stare in his direction. 'Are you questioning my professionalism?'

'Yes. No. No, of course not. I'm sorry,' he blustered, wondering how she had grabbed the upper hand in this conversation. He had called her here because he thought that by looking over her shoulder he could push this report through faster. But now he realised his mistake. She was a consummate professional. Summoning her here was going to do nothing but slow her down.

He was the one being unprofessional. There was no way that he would have accused someone of that if they didn't have a shared past. It was unforgivable for him to say that to Meena. 'I didn't mean it and I'm sorry,' he added. 'That was indefensible. I know you're a professional.'

'Good,' she said, uncrossing her arms and returning her gaze to the laptop, typing in a password and clicking through login screens. 'And thank you. Because annoying me isn't going to get this finished any faster, you know. I've told you that before.'

'I know. I should have listened. It's just, the last time we spoke…'

She took a deep breath and he saw her brace herself.

'Last time we spoke was very awkward,' she confirmed. 'We spoke about stuff from the past that probably should have stayed there. I'd prefer it if we didn't speak about it again.'

'Fine by me.'

Perfect by him, in fact, he thought, letting out a long, relieved breath. He had never wanted to talk about it in the first place. He never would have if she hadn't pushed him so hard. Now that it was out there, the best thing that they could both do was ignore it and push it back into the sealed box where it belonged.

But he was surprised, nonetheless. Because Meena was the one who had pushed and pushed him to reveal their past—and, now that she knew, she had decided she wasn't interested any more? The last thing that he wanted was to rake over it all again, but he couldn't deny that he was surprised that she had dropped the subject entirely.

Maybe it was him, he mused. He had been giving off signals that he wasn't good for her from the moment that he had met her. He couldn't blame her for taking notice of them and deciding to wipe their relationship from her memory—voluntarily this time.

Meena talked him through the report from their last dive and her updated plans for the reef off Le Bijou. He couldn't fault her work. Her research was precise, and her plans for the project detailed and thorough. As far as he could see, the only remaining question mark over the permits were these bloody turtles.

'Will you definitely see the turtles hatch tonight?' he asked her when they reached the end of the report.

'I've learned not to get too hung up on "definitely",' she replied, annoyingly obtuse.

'Okay, do you think that you *will* see them tonight, then?'

She shrugged. 'I hope so. But I hoped that last night too.'

'You were on Le Bijou last night?'

'I camped on the beach,' she said. Her words sparked a host of memories, of the night that they had camped out, their two blankets on the sand doing less to keep them warm than the heat of one another's bodies. They'd made a small fire, eaten sticky mangoes and then watched the stars appear one by one in the sky.

'What?' Meena asked, and he knew that some of what he had been remembering must have shown on his face.

'It's nothing,' he said quickly, trying to cover his tracks. Cover his feelings.

'A memory?' she asked.

He hesitated. She was the one who had said they should leave the past where it was. But he had promised not to lie to her.

'Yes.' Monosyllables were safest.

'Ours?'

He nodded. 'Yes.'

'Le Bijou?'

'Yes, Le Bijou.' He cracked; holding these memories himself was too much of a responsibility. She had shared in the making of them, and she was as entitled to them as he was. He could talk about Le Bijou without talking about how he had felt for her. He could give her something without giving her *everything*. 'We spent the night there,' he said simply, leaving out the details.

Meena looked thoughtful.

'We went there a lot?' she asked.

He could have ignored the question. He had promised not to lie; he hadn't promised always to answer every question. But the look on her face, the eagerness for new information, meant that he couldn't deny her.

'Yes,' he said eventually. 'We went there a lot.'

It was where she had always felt safe since the accident. Where she had always been comfortable. Where she had eventually learned to be happy again. And now she knew that she had shared that place with him.

Was that why he had bought it? Because it had been special to them?

It would have been sweet, she thought, if he hadn't been bent on trying to destroy it. Despite her best efforts to limit the impact of the development, despite the relatively sensitive plans that Guy had submitted, her tranquil island retreat would never be the same once building began.

Was he trying to erase what had gone on there? What they had shared?

'Was that why you bought the island?' she asked, unsure of whether she would get an answer, never mind one that she would like.

'Yes.' Another monosyllable. Marvellous. Piecing together her history one syllable at a time wasn't remotely frustrating…

'Fine,' she said, her patience finally snapping. 'You don't have to tell me, Guy. You hoard those memories to yourself, and I'll pick up the crumbs and try and piece those few months together from the scraps that you throw me. It's not like I mean anything to you. I wouldn't expect you to try and understand.'

'It's not like that,' Guy protested.

'Four syllables this time. Lucky me.'

'I'm serious. You're better off not knowing. Trust me.'

'Trust you?' She raised her eyebrows in disbelief. 'And what possible reason have you given me to do that? What I know about you can be summed up in a handful of paragraphs, and the fact is that we had sex and you no longer care. That's fine. But this isn't just about that for me. Can't you see? I can't pretend that I don't care. I can't *not* care. Because to me that summer isn't about what happened between *us*. It's about *me*. It's about who I was. And the only clues that I have are the ones that you throw me, and I'm fed up of turning up here hoping for scraps and having to deal with your attitude to get them. Either start sharing our history with me or stop calling, Guy. It's not fair to trap me between the two.'

Guy let out a long breath, then came over and sat opposite her.

'We spent a lot of time on Le Bijou,' he confirmed, letting out another long breath. 'It was special to both of us.'

'And that's why you bought the island?' she asked. He nodded. 'And that's why you are intent on destroying it?'

His head snapped round to look at her. 'I'm not destroying it.'

'You're building a hotel on it. It'll never be the same again. It's hardly preserving it.'

'Fine, yes. I wanted to destroy it.'

She sat and looked at him for a long moment, the impact of that statement hitting.

'You hate it that much?'

Guy sighed, shaking his head. 'I don't hate it,' he said.

'Then why?'

'Because while it's sitting there, just as I—we—left it, I couldn't stop thinking about it.'

Meena felt the silence settle uncomfortably between them before she spoke again.

'It was that bad?' she asked, her voice soft.

'Bad. Good. I don't know.'

Meena was seriously starting to regret pulling on this thread. Answers were meant to be reassuring, but she wasn't liking the sound of where this was going. She thought again about what Guy had said—how he had kept the truth from her in order to protect her—and wondered if she had made a mistake in pushing for it.

'Did you really leave because your holiday was over?' she asked, not sure that she wanted the answer. But, now they had started, she wanted everything out in the open. She wanted to know how bad it could get. And then once it was done, flushed out of her system, she could move on. She *would* move on.

He nodded, but she could see there was more, so she waited. 'It wasn't really a holiday. It was an apprenticeship. I was here to see how the resort worked, before I went back to head office in Sydney to work with my parents. We didn't have much of a choice about me leaving.'

'Did I want you to go?' she pressed. He fixed her with a stare, as if he was challenging her. He didn't want to tell her this, but she wasn't going to let him off the hook. This was her history too. She was entitled to know it.

'Yes,' he answered. She thought about that. Thought about where he'd been going back to. Thought about her scholarship to Australia, and her plans to continue her research there.

'Was I meant to come with you?' she asked.

It felt as if they were fixed in this space between her question and his answer for days. Until eventually he nodded, his eyes dropping from hers, staring out at the water. 'Yes.'

This time, she could forgive him the monosyllable. 'I never came,' she said, her voice full of sadness. Sad for him. Sad for herself. Sad for the fact she was having to ask Guy these intensely personal questions; that she couldn't know the answers for herself.

He shook his head and shrugged. 'And now I know why. It wasn't anyone's fault.'

She traced the line of a scar under her hair, almost without realising what she was doing.

'You never knew,' she said, her voice low. 'You never knew why I didn't follow you?'

No wonder he had seemed so angry with her, she thought. She had assumed all this time that she was the one who had been abandoned. When she'd been working through her recovery and rehabilitation, she had wondered where her lover was. How he could be moving on with his life while she was left with a devastated body and a broken heart, even though she didn't know the cause. To find out that she had hurt Guy just as badly winded her.

'I'm sorry,' she said. 'That must have been hard for you.'

'It was a long time ago,' he replied, which didn't really answer her question. 'Are we going to discuss the dive?' Guy continued, dragging their conversation back to the professional.

'I'm not sure that this conversation is finished,' Meena said, sensing his barriers flying back up but hoping that she might get some more information out of him if she trod carefully.

'It is for me,' Guy replied, his eyes hard.

Part of Meena bristled, wanting to push back, demand her answers. But she could see that Guy would not be receptive.

She thought again about how it must have been for him—waiting to hear from her, assuming that she had made up her mind not to come to him. And then he had turned up here and found that she had no memory of him. She decided not to push. Not just now. If she did, he was just going to clam up. And if that happened, and he decided to put more distance between them, she might never find out everything that she wanted.

'Fine, let's get to work, then,' she said, pulling up the relevant files on her laptop and talking him through her findings from their dive. He nodded along as she pointed out what she had recorded and the adjustments that would be needed at Le Bijou as a result.

'And once we have an answer about the turtles on the beach, I can finish my reports,' she said at last.

He let out a long sigh, and she could practically feel his relief.

'And you're going tonight?' he asked. 'To see the turtles?'

She nodded. 'Yes. I'd hoped to see them last night— we're so close to the end of the possible incubation period—but nothing happened. It's been sixty days since I found the nest, so I'm hoping something happens tonight. If it doesn't…' She didn't even want to think about what it would mean if she didn't see any hatchlings.

'You were out there *alone* last night?' Guy asked sharply, and Meena didn't know quite what to make of his tone.

'Of course,' she replied, trying to keep any hint of annoyance out of her voice, but bristling all the same from his questioning how she did her job or how she took care of herself. Either way, it was none of his business.

Guy narrowed his eyes. 'Why "of course"?'

'Who did you think I would take with me?'

'I don't care who you take,' Guy said with a nonchalance that stung. 'I just don't think you should be out there all night on your own.'

She crossed her arms and stared him down in a way that was starting to feel familiar. 'It's not a big deal, Guy,' she told him, hoping that he would pick up from her tone that she didn't care for his input on this matter.

'I don't care. I don't like it.'

The message obviously had not been received. 'Well, then,' Meena said, wanting this conversation to be at an end. 'It's a good job it's not your decision, then, isn't it?'

'You work for me,' Guy said, his words eerily cool.

Meena leaned forward and rested her elbows on the desk, fixing him with an equally cold stare and hoping that he couldn't see how her heart was racing in her chest.

'When the permits are approved,' she said, making her words deliberately slow, 'I will be considering whether to come and work for your company. Right now, I work for the government of St Antoine. I don't report to you, no matter how much you like to call and demand my presence.'

Guy huffed. 'I do not do that.'

'Then what am I doing here?' she asked, a false note of sweetness in her voice.

'You're working.'

'Right, because I couldn't possibly update you over email. Or the phone.'

'It's easier this way,' Guy stated, as if the strength of his opinion could make it fact.

Meena snapped the lid of her laptop shut and started to gather up her papers. 'For you, maybe,' she said, knowing that Guy would get the subtext.

He stayed silent long enough for her to break her resolve and turn and look at him, wondering what he was plotting. 'Look, Meena, I'm sorry for annoying you. I was just concerned about you being on the island on your own overnight.'

'You don't need to be.'

'Well, I am.' He was back to monosyllables, but they were softer than they had been before—less combative—and Meena felt her shoulders relax down from her ears a fraction in response to his change in tone.

'I'm sorry you feel that way, Guy. But there's not a lot you can do about it. Like I said, I need to get this job done, and this is how I work. You're not my boss, and you're not my boyfriend. You can't stop me.'

His forehead creased in the way that Meena knew meant he was plotting something. 'I can come with you,' he said.

She laughed—couldn't help herself. 'Oh, right, the great Guy Williams camping out on a beach waiting to see turtle babies. I can really see that happening.'

'It's happening. I already told you, I've done it before.'

She stopped and stared at him for a moment. 'You're not serious. That was a million years ago.'

'It was seven years ago and I'm deadly serious. I'm not letting you stay out there alone.'

'Letting me? You wouldn't have got away with talking to me like that when we were together, Guy. Never mind now. No one "lets" me do anything.'

'How do you know how I spoke to you when we were together?'

It was a low blow and it hurt—a lot. He was right. She didn't know. Perhaps when she'd met him she'd turned into the sort of woman who had done as she was told, gone along with what he had wanted. Perhaps that was how she had ended up pregnant. But, even as she had the thought, she dismissed it. That wasn't who she was. It wasn't who she had ever been, and meeting Guy wouldn't—couldn't—have changed that.

'I just know, okay? I might not remember you, or us. But I know myself, Guy, and I would never stand for that.'

A small smile betrayed Guy.

'You're right,' he said, the smile creasing his eyes. 'You never did.'

'So stop trying it on now.' She tried to be cross, but his smile was contagious and she could feel it softening her features even as she tried schooling them into something stern.

'I'm not trying to force anything, Meena. I would love to keep you company on Le Bijou tonight, with the added bonus of knowing that you are safe. Am I welcome to come and watch for the turtles with you?'

She sat in silence while she considered the proposition. Truth be told, she hadn't been all that happy about sleeping out on Le Bijou alone and she would have been grateful for some company. More important, if Guy came along tonight, spent more time on Le Bijou, maybe he would soften his plans for the development. If he remembered how special the island was, he might rein in his development plans, so they made less of an impact on the environment of Le Bijou. Perhaps he would even abandon the plans altogether.

'Fine. You can come along,' she said eventually. 'But bring your own tent.'

CHAPTER SEVEN

SHE HAD DECLINED Guy's offer to bring his yacht to the island. She didn't want it anchored off shore, not knowing what impact it might have on the marine life. Her little boat had been puttering around Le Bijou for so long that it felt like part of the ecosystem, and it was perfectly capable of getting them to and from the island, even if it lacked a bit in the luxury stakes. She had half-expected Guy to pull a face when she had insisted that they both use it, but if he had been annoyed he hadn't shown it.

Instead he had turned up at the marina wearing a casual pair of cargo shorts and a polo shirt with a stuffed rucksack on his back. She could see a tent and a sleeping bag, and was glad that he had taken her instructions seriously. She'd meant what she'd said about not sharing.

Even with separate tents, though, this was probably not one of her best ideas, she thought as she steered them up to the little jetty and tied up her boat. Guy scrambled out first and held out a hand to help her up, and she hesitated before she took it. But it was just a polite gesture, she told herself as she made herself reach out for it, trying to ignore the zing that she felt when his fingers touched hers. They walked over to where she had set up camp the night before and pitched the tents quickly. The sun was setting fast, shadows growing long around them as she knocked tent pegs into the earth and tightened the lines. She was unrolling her sleeping bag when she felt Guy's eyes on her back and turned to find him watching her.

With the setting sun behind him, she couldn't make out his expression. He was just a dark silhouette against the bleeding orange of the sun dipping into the water.

'What is it?' she asked as the last rays of sunlight streaked around them.

'It's...' Guy hesitated, as if he was making up his mind whether to speak. 'It's just strange, being back here again,' he said eventually, coming round to the front of the tents and spreading a blanket on the ground. 'We spent so much time here before. And I've had this place in my mind for so long.'

'It's so strange not being able to remember it,' Meena said, sitting on the blanket and wondering whether this conversation would have been different if she'd had her memories. If Guy would even have talked about the past at all if she hadn't been reliant on him to fill in the missing parts for her.

'It's strange for me too,' Guy said, lit now only by the full moon as he dropped down beside her. Darkness had fallen fast, and Meena didn't want to risk interfering with the natural instincts of the turtles by turning on a torch or lighting a fire. 'It's hard to know what to tell you.'

'I want to know it all,' she said, glad of the darkness that hid her expression, letting her ask questions she'd never have dared to if she'd properly had to look him in the eye.

'I know...' Guy said. 'I know you think that you do, but...'

'But what? But you know what I want better than I do?'

'But me telling you isn't the same as you remembering.' He explained his thinking. 'Would it really change anything?'

'It might,' she countered. He could never know what it was like for her to live with this hole in her memories. To feel as if she didn't know herself. 'I want to know everything I can about that time when my memories are missing.'

He sighed, shaking his head. 'Why does it mean so much to you? It all happened such a long time ago. Why can't we just leave it all in the past?'

How could he ask that? Had their relationship meant so little to him that he could just pretend that it had never happened in the first place? Had she meant so little to him?

She could see why it wouldn't matter to him. He was clearly a womaniser who picked up women and dropped them with barely a thought for what came next. But she wasn't like that. Had he known, then, that she'd been a virgin? She couldn't think of anything more mortifying to ask. If he hadn't known, it would be mortifying telling him now. That he had been so special to her when she had clearly meant nothing to him.

'Because I deserve to know my own past,' she told him. 'You're hoarding these memories like it's your decision only. But I helped make those memories, and I think I'm entitled to have them back. Perhaps not everyone with amnesia feels this way. But what I've pieced together of that summer doesn't make sense. The Meena that I see through those memories doesn't make sense to me. I want to understand her. Want to understand who I was.'

'I don't remember you changing,' he said, as if that was the end of the matter. How could it be? How could she have been pregnant with his baby if she hadn't become someone else over those months?

'That's not possible,' she said eventually. 'I know that I changed. I want to know why.'

'Is this because—?' Guy stopped himself, and that was all she needed to hear to know that he was about to tell her something important.

'Just say it,' she told him.

He hesitated, but she knew that her tone hadn't given him any choice but to answer. He must remember something of her, to know that. 'Is it because of me? Because of our relationship. Is that what you're confused about?'

'Partly,' she confirmed, though she couldn't tell him about the baby. Assuming that he didn't already know, of course. It was impossible trying to pick through these conversations when both of them were hiding so much. Surely if he had known then that she was pregnant he would have asked about it by now?

But even if it hadn't been for the baby she would still have been confused about what had happened. The Meena that she remembered wouldn't have slept with Guy. So she must have been someone different those months.

'I just don't understand...*us*,' she said at last, not sure that it was a good idea mentioning their relationship, but unsure of how else to get the answers that she needed. 'The me that I remember wouldn't have...' She was grateful for the dark hiding her expression. If she'd done it, she should be able to talk about it. But as she didn't even remember having sex with him—having sex with anyone—she figured that it didn't count.

'Wouldn't have slept with me?' Guy asked outright.

The blood rushed furiously to her face and she could feel her skin burning even as the evening was starting to turn cooler.

'Yes,' she said, forcing out the word to break the awkward silence.

'I know that you hadn't before,' he said after a long pause. 'That I was your first.'

She kept thinking that it wasn't possible to be any more embarrassed than she already was, and then Guy would go and open his mouth and suddenly she was dying all over again.

'It wasn't a casual thing,' he went on when her silence continued. 'If that's what you were thinking. It was important to you. To both of us.'

She blew out a breath, hoping that it would take the

heat in her face with it. 'I... I'm glad. That helps,' she told him. And she meant it. It was a relief, if she was honest, to know that it had been important enough to her for Guy to know that. They must have talked about it, for him just to come out and say it like that. And he still knew her, to know that that was what she was wondering.

It was so strange, she acknowledged, the asymmetry of their relationship. He knew so much about their past. But they had both made so many assumptions, got so much wrong, that their last few years hadn't been so different really. They must both have been wondering what had happened to the person who they had loved that summer. She must have been as much a mystery to Guy as he had been to her.

And she was keeping a secret too, a huge one. Because Guy hadn't mentioned anything about the pregnancy. She was demanding honesty from him but couldn't offer it in return and she couldn't pretend that that didn't make her uncomfortable. But if he didn't know... She thought of the pain that she had felt, finding out that she'd lost a baby. And she'd not even had any context for that knowledge. She hadn't known whose baby it was. Hadn't known whether she had been happy or anxious to know that she was pregnant. Hadn't known how she had felt about the father.

Guy had all that.

That baby would have a meaning to Guy that she might never be able to understand. And she had a choice about whether or not he should know. An option that had never been open to her—to keep something from him that could only hurt him. She had been angry when she'd realised that Guy had been doing the same thing to her, hiding things that he thought would hurt her, but, faced with telling him about the baby that they had lost, she knew why he had made that decision. Who would choose to deliberately hurt the person that they cared about? Especially if it was all in the past. If there was nothing that they could do about it.

She could spare him that.

She didn't want to think too hard about why it seemed so important to her to protect Guy from pain. What that meant about how she felt about him. It could be purely human compassion, she considered, but knew that she was lying to herself. Regardless of the reason, she knew that she would do it. She would carry the memory of their baby by herself as the only person in the world who knew and cared that that life had existed, even for such a short time. She would treasure it, keep it safe, and she would spare Guy the agony of imagining what might have been, as she had so many times over the years.

Or at least she wished that it could be as simple as that. But it could never be, not between them. She sat on the ground beside Guy and looked out over the water.

'Do you want to hear more?' Guy asked, both their eyes fixed on the reflection of the moon on the gentle waves of the sea, the hush and swoosh of the water over the sand the only other noise in the night.

'Yes,' she breathed, wondering how much of her history she was going to rediscover tonight.

'We sat here,' Guy said, something wistful and distant in his voice. 'Right here. We camped, just like tonight.'

Meena held her breath, wondering how far this was going to go.

'We'd been struggling to find somewhere to meet,' Guy continued. 'You were living at home with your parents. We didn't want to meet anywhere in the re-sort, because we were worried about your boss find-ing out. It wasn't worth risking your job over. So we came out here, in your boat.' He fell silent, staring out over the water, and she wondered if that was it. If that was all he was going to tell her.

'That was the first time,' he went on, and she knew exactly which *first time* he was talking about.

She felt a shiver completely at odds with the still sweltering temperature.

'We'd been...close...before. But that night...was something else.'

He didn't say it, and he didn't have to. She knew ex-actly what he meant. She could almost feel it. Flashes of memories, or dreams, came back to her. His hands were on her beneath her sweatshirt. Her heart was beating faster, her breath coming shorter, and heat was rising in every part of her body.

Was that real? she wondered for the millionth time. Were those real memories, pulled up from a deep, damaged part of her brain that she couldn't reach when she was awake? Or were they pure fantasy, drawing only on an overactive imagination and out-of-control libido? That was one answer she'd never get, she sup-posed. Guy couldn't tell her what it had been like to be her in that moment. What she might have felt for him. How she might have felt when he had been inside her.

She looked out over the water, wondering if he was remembering it as she was. Or as she was trying to. Could he remember the touch of her fingers on his skin? The feel of the sand beneath them, the rush of the waves their soundtrack?

And then she remembered that he wanted to destroy everything that he remembered about this island. He was going to build a generic luxury resort here, in the place that he told her had once been so special to them, and it was like ice down her spine.

That was how much it meant to him, she reminded herself. The night that he was recalling here. He wanted to pour concrete over it, bury it. Destroy it, so that he no longer had to be troubled by it.

She must remember that, she told herself. They hadn't come out here tonight to reminisce. They were here to complete her environmental survey so that Guy could continue with his work of building over everything that they had shared here.

'It was a long time ago,' she said, hearing the frost in her voice and wondering if Guy would recognise it. Had he had cause to hear it back then, she wondered, or had everything always been happy between them? A simple summer romance that never would have weathered the slightest storm. 'I suppose it doesn't matter any more. I don't want to hear anything else,' she said.

Despite what she'd said about having to fill in the gaps, the reminder that Guy wanted to destroy those memories took the shine off any new information. The past was important, but so was the present. And she shouldn't get confused between the two. She was in danger of doing that, she realised. That was why Guy had wanted to keep this from her, after all. Because he assumed that if she knew what had been between them in the past she wouldn't be able to keep herself from bringing that relationship into the present. From expecting him to act like someone who had loved her, rather than someone she simply had to work with. He had been right. She had to remember the boundaries between them.

'It *was* a long time ago,' Guy said, still sounding thoughtful. 'But, sitting out here like this, I guess it doesn't feel that way.'

Her gaze shot across to his, trying to catch the expression on his face in the moonlight. What was that supposed to mean?

'Well, that's the point of bulldozing this place, I guess,' she reminded him. 'So you don't have to remember any more.'

He sighed and shook his head.

'I thought that was what I wanted.'

Meena held her breath, waiting for him to say something more, to explain, but he didn't. She couldn't leave it at that, though.

'Does that mean it's not what you want now?' she asked hesitantly, not sure whether she wanted the answer.

'I'd forgotten how it felt to sit here like this,' he said on a sigh. 'To be the only people on this island. To be so alone, in a good way. All I could think about was… what had come after.'

'When you were alone in a bad way?'

'Yeah.' He nodded. 'I thought that I didn't want this place to exist any more. But I'm not sure that that's true now. I think… I didn't want it to exist if I couldn't have it.'

'Guy, we're not—'

'It feels petty now,' he interrupted her. 'And I don't want to be petty. What we had was special. Even though it's over, it doesn't mean I have to tear through here to try and assuage my ego.'

'I don't think you're being petty,' she said gently.

'You don't think I'm doing the right thing,' he countered. There was an edge to his voice that hinted at self-reproach.

'I don't,' she agreed, surprised at the self-awareness Guy was offering. She hadn't expected this tonight. Hadn't expected him to be honest with her about how painful he found their past. She had assumed that she had meant little to him. But if that were true he wouldn't be hurting like this now. 'I don't think you're doing the right thing. But that doesn't mean I think you're being petty. I think you were hurt, and you had every reason to feel that way. You thought that this would make you feel better. But I don't think it will.'

'I don't know any more,' he said. 'But it's too late now anyway.'

Meena shook her head. 'Please don't say that. It doesn't have to be, not for Le Bijou.'

He looked at her, surprised. 'You don't understand my business, Meena. It's not as simple as you think.'

'No,' she said simply. 'I don't understand. But I know that no harm has been done yet—you could stop this, if you wanted to.'

'I never said that I wanted to.'

Meena sat up a little straighter at the bite in his tone. She had thought that they were getting on better, and here was the payoff, she guessed. He opened up and then snapped back shut when he realised what he had done.

'Guy, if all this has been to punish me, then consider it done, okay? Even the thought of what you're planning to do here breaks my heart. Is that enough? Will you stop now?'

'It isn't about punishing you, Meena. It was never about that.'

'Then what? Because whatever you think, this is punishing me. It's hurting me. And I don't believe you think that it's the right thing to do.' She held his gaze, refusing to let him look away, challenging him to tell her that she was wrong.

'You tell me what the right thing to do is, then,' he replied at last. 'Because I've already sunk millions of dollars into this development. I have a whole team waiting to get started on it. You tell me what I'm supposed to tell them. That I've changed my mind because I've been reminiscing with an old girlfriend?'

'If you think I'd care about what you're going to tell them, or about the money, Guy, you don't know me as well as you think you do.'

He huffed out a small laugh, breaking the tension between them. 'I didn't think you'd care about that at all, actually.'

She managed a small smile, pleased that the atmosphere was gradually easing. 'Do you mean it?' she asked. 'Would you really stop it, if you could?'

'It's not that simple.'

'We don't have to decide anything tonight,' Meena reminded him, not wanting the conversation to turn hostile again. 'We're meant to be watching for the hatchlings.'

'I'd almost forgotten,' Guy acknowledged.

Meena fixed her eyes on the sand, looking and listening intently for any sign of activity on the beach.

Guy moved closer, so they were sharing the same line of sight down to the beach, and she was hyper aware of the heat of his body beside her. Her own skin was still stickily warm, and the knowledge that Guy was so close was doing nothing to cool it.

'Does it help?' Guy asked, settling beside her, his gaze following hers out over the sand towards the water. 'Knowing more about what happened?' His voice was soft, almost sensuous, and Meena repressed a shiver.

'It helps,' she agreed, intensely aware of the heat of his body beside her, the bulk of him. It seemed so familiar from her dreams, as if she could strip his shirt off and know every line of his body from memory. He turned and caught her looking. She held his gaze, caught in the stream of energy that seemed to flow between them. It must have been because they were talking about their past, she thought. That was what had charged the atmosphere like this. There was definitely something between them, something pulling her towards him, that hadn't been there before.

Or maybe it had just been easier to ignore it before, when they hadn't been talking about the fact that she had lost her virginity to him, perhaps in this very spot.

'What are you thinking?' Guy asked.

'Nothing,' she replied, though she didn't look away. Didn't break the connection between them.

That look she was giving him was dangerous.

It was knowing.

It shouldn't be—she'd told him that she couldn't remember being with him, but that was not what her face was telling him. He knew that look; he remembered it well. It was the look she got when she was thinking about sex. About him. He should know. He'd seen it often enough. Looked for it, in fact, knowing that they could share a heated look and then she would seek him out later and find a way for them to sneak off together and meet somewhere. That look had led them to this island once. And here they were again, Meena with that look on her face, though he knew that she couldn't remember what they'd shared here.

'I don't believe you,' he said with a smile that he couldn't help forming, regardless of the danger they were heading towards. 'Tell me.'

She didn't have to. He knew that she was perfectly capable of ignoring his command. It was a question of whether she wanted to share with him. He wasn't sure that he wanted her to. Whether that was a good idea.

'I don't know,' Meena said. 'I have these…images… in my head, and I don't know if they're real or if I'm making them up.'

'Why don't you tell me what they are? I'll tell you if they're real.'

'I—I can't,' she said, and he knew that he had been right. She was thinking about sex. Which was interesting on so many fronts. Had she remembered something? If she had, that was huge. From what she'd told him, they would be the first memories that she'd recovered of that time before her accident. And if they weren't really memories, if it was her imagination, that meant that she was fantasising about him. About them together. And that meant that their past was still very much in the present. He could feel it between them. How could he not when she was positively humming with sexual energy?

'They can't be memories,' she said, shaking her head, her voice uncertain.

'Why not?' Surely there was the possibility that her memories could return. She'd acknowledged that to him before.

'Because I don't have any memories!' she stated. 'These are just…flashes. Feelings.' Her voice trailed off, but he couldn't leave this unfinished. It didn't matter that he knew that he was leading them towards danger.

'About me?' he asked.

She narrowed her eyes, clearly fighting with herself about whether to answer honestly. Or at all.

'Yes, about you.' She paused. 'Always about you,'

she added with a sigh. Her body softened beside him and he ached to draw her into his arms. He could see the toll that it was taking on her, not knowing their past. Searching for memories that her brain couldn't access. He knew how much strength it was taking her to ask him to fill those missing memories for her.

'What about me?' Guy asked. She needed this. She wanted this. Wanted to know the answers to these questions.

He knew that he was strolling into danger. But he couldn't help it. Couldn't stop himself. Out here, on this beach, on *their* beach, knowing that Meena was running X-rated fantasies of them through her mind, looking for clues that might tell her if they were real, the real world felt too far away. It could have been that night. It could have been the night that they had come out here and lain on a blanket just like this one, and she had loved and trusted him, and he had been deserving of that love.

While they were here, he could make himself believe that he was that man again, *could* be that man again. That he could be deserving of her trust.

He turned to her at the same moment as she turned to him, and suddenly she was closer to him than she had been for the past seven years.

His eyes never left hers as his arm curved around her back, watching for any sign that she wanted him to stop. Hoping that she would be the one to be sensible and put a stop to this, because he wasn't sure that he could. His other hand still rested on the soft, worn cotton of the blanket they had spread on the sand beneath them. Meena's eyes drifted closed and he watched those long, thick lashes as they brushed against her skin before she opened them again. When she met his gaze this time, there was something new in her expression. A determination and a fearlessness that he had seen before.

He sighed, smiled. Knowing that he was lost. Helpless, as he always had been with Meena.

She leaned in, those eyelashes sweeping shut again as she closed the distance between them. His hand came up to cup her cheek, holding her just before that moment when their lips would meet. Wanting to stretch this moment, to soak in it. In the promise of everything that was to come. To stretch that moment before their lives became so much more complicated.

Their first kiss hadn't been so considered. It had been furiously hot, between two young, inexperienced kids who had no idea what they were getting themselves into.

He couldn't launch himself in blind this time. He knew too much for that. Knew where this could lead. Knew how good this was going to be.

And with that memory he groaned, slipped his hand through the thick curls of her hair and brought her mouth to his.

At the first touch of her lips, he wanted to explode. To push her back on the soft cotton of the blanket and show her exactly what they had been missing out on for the last seven years. Instead, he shut off his imagination and channelled every firing neuron into the present moment. To fully experiencing the subtle friction of her lips. To hearing every nuance of the moan that escaped her as his tongue touched hers for the first time. His hand reached for the soft curve of her waist and he schooled it to stay gentle. To ignore the impulse begging him to squeeze her hard. To wrap both arms tight around her waist and never let her go. He dragged himself back to the present, drowning in the smell of her hair, the soft give of her flesh beneath his hands, and wasn't sure he would ever be able to stop.

They had to stop, Meena thought as she reached for Guy's shirt to pull him in tighter. She'd thought that this could be a simple test, to see whether her fantasies were based on reality or entirely constructed in her mind. But as soon as he had touched her, pushing her hair behind her ear and cupping her jaw, she'd known that this was so much more than that. This was her giving in to every temptation of the past week. Every time she had fantasised about this man had led them to this moment.

But they had to stop. She hesitated, and it was enough to break the spell. Guy lifted his head and looked at her, his expression as shocked as she felt by what had just happened.

'I...' he started, and she was touched to see that he was as affected by the kiss as she was.

'It's fine,' she interrupted, speaking quickly. 'I'm sure it was just nostalgia getting the better of us,' she added, trying to explain away what had just happened between them, though she was still feeling drunk from it. The last thing that she needed was Guy thinking that she thought that a relationship between them would be a good idea. How could it be, when she didn't even know who she was? When being around Guy made her act in a way that meant she didn't even recognise herself?

Guy stared at her for a beat longer than was comfortable, as if he didn't believe what she was saying.

'Nostalgia,' he repeated.

'Or curiosity. Maybe both,' she added quickly, aware that she was rambling. 'We should just forget about it,' she added, hoping that they could finish this conversation before she died of embarrassment.

That kiss had been hot. Seriously hot. But also seriously confusing. Because her and Guy were in the past. Were meant to be in the past. He had made that completely clear from the minute she had forced him to confess that they even had a history. He had made it abundantly clear that he had no interest in rekindling what they had once had. Well, until he had kissed her.

She had seen his expression when they had talked about how she had never come to him in Australia. It didn't matter that she had been in a coma at the time. He had been hurt, and it was perfectly evident from the expression on his face that he hadn't forgiven her. Couldn't forget. Probably never would, if he hadn't by now.

And she didn't want to be with him either. Couldn't be with him. She was still trying to find out who she was. Who she had been. She had thought that being around Guy would help with that. That he could fill in those parts of her past that she couldn't remember herself. But she had been wrong. Because, when she was around him, she barely recognised herself. In the past fifteen minutes, she had done things that she had never done before—or probably had, but she didn't remember. And that was the point. The way she reacted to Guy was so unlike her that she couldn't deal with it. She didn't need that reminder that there were vast parts of herself that she just didn't understand.

'So,' Guy said, edging away from her subtly, just enough that her breathing could slow to a normal rate, and pulling his arm back from around her waist, crossing it over his body. 'These turtles...'

They sat on the beach for hours, the silence between them becoming more and more strained as the time passed. By the time the sun began to rise and she realised that the hatchlings weren't going to appear, the atmosphere was so charged that she was surprised neither of them had spontaneously combusted.

It would be better tomorrow, she told herself. The sunlight would wash away the memories of that kiss, they would climb into her little boat and they would leave what had happened on the island safely on the island.

CHAPTER EIGHT

HOW COULD HE have been so stupid? Guy thought to himself as Meena navigated them around the coral reefs and away from Le Bijou. Since the first moment he had laid eyes on her again he'd known one thing above all else—he could not get involved with her. He would not be in a relationship again. Not with her, not with anyone. He had already proved that a relationship with him brought nothing but pain and danger, and he wasn't going to put anyone else at risk.

In the time that they had been apart, he had turned into someone who no longer deserved Meena. He had to protect her more than anyone because their shared past and her amnesia made her vulnerable. It had been unforgivable of him to forget that last night. He should never have let himself kiss her, however tempted he had been. It only went to prove his point. He knew that getting involved with her would only ever lead to her getting hurt, and yet he'd done it anyway. He'd kissed her, knowing that he could never be with her. If she hadn't stopped him, God only knew how far it would have gone before he'd come to his senses. If he'd been able to. He'd never been one for self-control around Meena before.

And now she wouldn't even meet his eye. She was the one who had written the whole thing off as curiosity or nostalgia, but she didn't entirely mean it. That much was clear from the way that she was avoiding his gaze. The way that she had jumped a mile when his hand had brushed hers when he'd helped her pack away the tent. In the strained silence between them now, as he looked out over the water, or up at the clear blue sky, or anywhere but into her curious brown eyes.

Well, this was the final part of the environmental survey, so as long as she approved the permits he could be off the island and back in Sydney in just a matter of days.

He was blindsided by the wrench that he felt as he had that thought. A pain that reminded him of the heartbreak he had felt those years ago when he had said goodbye to Meena before. Back then, he had at least been able to tell himself that he would see her soon, when she flew out to Australia to continue her research. But she'd never come, and his heart had cracked and then broken for good. And, when he'd turned to drink and partying to numb the pain, someone had died.

Now he was back here, feeling more of that pain, and wondering whether it was possible for him to be any more broken.

Meena looked over her reports, desperately trying to keep her head in the present and stop her thoughts drifting back to last night on the beach. She was a professional. She had a responsibility to her position to give this environmental survey the consideration that it deserved. She couldn't let her personal feelings for the applicant, or her memories of the area in question, colour her judgement.

Despite all her hopes, no turtles had hatched last night. She'd been keeping an eye on the spot every day since she'd seen the tracks which looked like they were leading to a nest. Legally she had to wait a week to excavate the nest and find out what had happened. Maybe she'd missed the hatchlings somehow? But she knew that she hadn't. The nest hadn't produced any live young.

It had been the last certain thing that she could think of to delay this development. If there were turtles nesting on the beach, producing live hatchlings, she could have used that to put a stop to it, or at least stall for more time. Without it, what did they have? The bleaching to the coral might be enough, perhaps. But, perversely, her successes with reviving reefs elsewhere made that argument weaker. And she wasn't sure that her bosses would consider that enough of a reason to reject the applications.

She would try, though.

She drummed her pencil on the draft of the report as she thought it over, but her mind wouldn't leave alone the memories of last night. When she closed her eyes, she could see Guy's face, bent towards her, the second before his lips met hers. She could smell the salt of the sea and the unique scent of Guy as their bodies had pressed together. She could feel the soft, cool cotton of the blanket beneath her bare legs, and hear the gasp of their breath as they'd broken off the kiss.

Memories. All real. And the sensations were so close to those that she had dreamed that she could no longer write them off as mere fantasy.

They shouldn't have done it. It was clear to her that Guy did not want a relationship. And she couldn't see how she could let someone into her life when she was still so unsure of who she was. When she had so many unanswered questions about her past. There was no chance of her being able to commit to another person—or of wanting to—when she did not even know herself.

No, last night was a mistake, and they would be foolish to repeat it. But they had both known that it was foolish last night and that hadn't stopped them.

She added a couple of lines to the report and then considered the options on the screen in front of her. Accept or reject. There was no grey area where this computer program was concerned. If she rejected the application, Guy would not get his permits. He could appeal the decision with revised plans, or he could forget the idea of building on Le Bijou altogether.

He had hinted last night that that was what he had wanted.

She shook her head. She couldn't let that influence her. This had to be based on the facts. The evidence. The science.

Meena looked up at the sound of the heavy knock on her office door and started when she saw Guy standing there. His face was drawn into hard lines, and she swallowed, nervous for a moment before she squared her shoulders and stood, refusing to let him intimidate her.

'Guy, what a—'

'What the hell is this, Meena?' he asked, brandishing a piece of paper.

She couldn't actually read it, with him waving it around, but she didn't have to be a genius to work out that he had received the email formally informing him that his planning applications had been rejected on environmental grounds.

'You tell me, Guy.'

'You rejected the application? Why?'

'The information is all there in the report. The potential harm to the environment of Le Bijou is too great. I couldn't approve the development.'

'But we've been working together on this, Meena, and you never suggested...'

'I never suggested what, Guy? That the application might not be successful? If that were the case then we wouldn't bother with a report at all. We would just rubber-stamp the application of every billionaire developer who happened to take an interest in our country.'

'Take an interest? What's that supposed to mean?'

'I didn't mean anything. What do you think it means?'

'I think it means that you're angry that I'm back. That I've chosen to develop an island that used to mean something to us. That you're letting our personal relationship cloud your judgement.'

Meena placed her hands on her hips. 'I wasn't aware that we have a personal relationship,' she stated, angry that he could accuse her.

'You know what I mean,' Guy said, grinding the words out. It was clear that he was as angry as she was. But she would not let that make her change her decision. 'Our history,' Guy continued. 'Our history on Le Bijou—that's why you rejected the application.'

Meena crossed her arms, not bothering to try to assuage her anger.

'You are accusing me of being unprofessional. It is not acceptable to come to my office and make those sorts of accusations. If you have a complaint, you can make it in writing,' she told him. Adding, 'To my boss,' to make her point. Guy was the one bringing their relationship into this. It had never been a part of her decision-making process. She'd only ever been thinking of Le Bijou, she told herself, and what was best for the ecosystem there. Never about him.

'Fine. I'll do that,' he said, turning for the door.

Meena was about to watch him walk out—storm out—without either of them mentioning that kiss on the island. Fine. It clearly meant nothing to him. But that wasn't the only thing that had happened that night. They had talked. Specifically, they had talked about the fact that Guy wasn't even sure that he wanted this development to go ahead.

'Guy...' she said, and he paused at the doorway. His shoulders dropped slightly, some of the tension leaving his body, and she guessed that his initial anger was fading along with the adrenaline that had no doubt fuelled his outburst.

'What?' His voice was still hard, though, the word pushed through a tense jaw and gritted teeth.

'If you wanted to stop the development…this would be a way.'

She knew that she was taking a risk, saying the words out loud. But she wanted him to know that he didn't have to fight this if he didn't want to. He could back out of the development gracefully, without losing face, if he accepted her report and didn't push back.

He stared at her, a muscle ticking in his jaw. 'You'll be hearing from me.'

Guy stalked out of her office and she collapsed back into her seat, trying to control the shake in her hands.

As the sound of Guy's footsteps faded down the hallway, she pulled up her emails and started drafting a note to her boss, reiterating why she had made the decision to deny the application and backing it all up with evidence. If Guy wanted to fight this, fine. She would treat it just as she would any other application. And that meant defending herself to her boss if her judgement was called into question.

She hadn't been expecting him to be so angry. Perhaps she should have… After that kiss, maybe he thought that she'd go easy on him. That he would get special treatment. Maybe that was why he had done it in the first place. But if that were the case, he was going to be sorely disappointed. Her only interest here was Le Bijou.

* * *

Guy sat on the deck of his yacht, willing away the shame that he felt at his outburst in Meena's office. He never should have accused her of being unprofessional. But he had been so shocked when he had received the email telling him that his application had been denied that he hadn't stopped to think. He had marched straight round to her office to have it out with her.

Would he have reacted that way if they hadn't kissed the last time that he had seen her? He couldn't deny that the kiss had affected him. He'd barely been able to think about anything else since it had happened.

So when Meena's name had popped up in his inbox he had thought, for a second, that maybe she wanted to talk about what had happened that night. He had thought that maybe *he* wanted to talk about what had happened that night, rather than give in to his instinct to ignore anything that came remotely close to emotional introspection. But then he'd read the message and understood that it had meant nothing to her. That she'd sent him this boilerplate message crushing all his plans for the island without even a single personal word to him.

Well, that told him everything that he needed to know about what she thought about that kiss. Good. He hadn't meant to kiss her anyway. And if she'd just been satisfying her curiosity then it had meant nothing to him either. There was no reason for either of them to mention the kiss, or their past together.

But he had to fight this ruling on the permits. So he had emailed her boss, knowing that it was a petty thing to do to Meena, calling her decision into question and asking that they reconsider.

When his phone rang, he was only half-surprised to see Meena's name on the screen. It was inevitable, really, that they would have to speak again in order to sort this out.

'Yes?' Guy asked, his voice tart and impersonal.

'Hello, Guy,' Meena said, and he winced at the formality in her voice. 'I've been asked to give you a call to see if we can reach a compromise on your application. My boss agrees that we cannot approve your plans as they are and has asked me to see if we can find a compromise. It may mean significantly altering your plans, if you are amenable to that.'

Amenable? He couldn't believe that just a few days ago he had sat on the beach with her in the moonlight, remembering the first time that they had made love, and had then shared a kiss so intensely emotional that it had been haunting him ever since. And now they were going to haggle over bureaucracy and blueprints. He wondered, not for the first time, if any of this was worth it. If he should just forget his plans completely and go back to Australia, where he would never have to see her again. Never be reminded of what they had had, and lost, on Le Bijou.

He shook his head, because he knew that was impossible. He'd tried it before. Tried burying those feelings. And it hadn't worked. That was why he'd come back in the first place. To try to do something different. To do something proactive to sully the memories he had of Le Bijou. And what had he done instead?

He'd made new memories. Made it harder than ever to forget.

'Fine,' he said eventually into his phone, because he was as determined as he had ever been to get this development built. 'Tomorrow. My office. Nine o'clock.'

'I can't make that, I'm afraid. I'll be excavating the possible nest on Le Bijou. But I can come afterwards.'

'No need. I'll meet you on Le Bijou.'

'Guy, I'm not sure that that's a good—'

'Nine o'clock. I'll see you there.'

CHAPTER NINE

MEENA WASN'T SURE what to expect when Guy's speedboat skittered to a stop the next morning. Would it be the fiery anger he'd shown her the last time they'd spoken in person, or the ice that she'd heard on the phone?

Well, either way, she was prepared for him. She had all her red lines drawn clearly in her mind for what would and would not be acceptable to the Environmental Agency. And if she could just find some evidence of live hatchlings this morning, even if they hadn't made it to the sea, that would be everything that she needed.

That was probably why Guy had invited himself along, she told herself. Nothing to do with what had happened the last time that they'd been on Le Bijou together. He probably just wanted to be sure she wasn't going to plant evidence or do something else nefarious with the nest.

She shuddered at the thought of having to compromise her ecological principles just because of Guy's money. She recognised that her superiors in the St Antoine government had their own priorities. But if she didn't speak to him about this, then someone else would. Quite probably someone who cared a lot less about damage being done to Le Bijou than she did. She couldn't trust anyone else to value the environment of that island as much as she herself did. So, as much as the idea of compromises pained her, she would be the one to make them.

Unless, of course, Guy had had a huge change of heart overnight and was prepared to scale back the resort to the point where it would no longer have a significant impact on the environment. Not likely, she acknowledged, preparing herself for a fight.

'Good morning, Guy,' she said as politely and formally as she could when he walked up the beach to where she was waiting for him, avoiding meeting his eye.

'Meena,' Guy said, nodding. 'Let's get on with it. I need to know what I finally have to do to get this report going my way.'

'What you need is plans that don't harm the environment of Le Bijou.' Meena didn't even look at him as she spoke. What was the point? It was the same thing that she had been saying for weeks. It wasn't her fault that Guy wasn't getting the message.

'Because this island is important to you,' Guy countered, trying to make this personal. She wasn't going to rise to it. She was here to do her job and that was the end of it. She dropped onto her knees on the sand and started digging carefully at the nest site, scooping sand with her hands, reaching further and further into it up to her wrist, then her elbow, until she was almost lying on the beach, her whole arm reaching into the sand.

'Because Le Bijou is protected by the government of St Antoine,' she pointed out, still looking down into the hole because she didn't trust herself to look at him.

'And that's the only reason you rejected the application?' Guy asked, still determined to make this about them rather than about her job. He had no right. 'Because I thought we had been working towards a solution.'

She couldn't answer. All she could think about now was the nest and why, after she had dug down so far that practically her whole arm was disappearing into the sand, she didn't have even a small piece of egg shell to show for it. She concentrated on widening the hole, wondering whether she had got the location wrong. Whether the marker she had used had moved somehow.

'I just find it strange that, just a couple of days after we kiss, you decide that you're not granting the permits after all,' Guy said.

Well, she wasn't rising to the bait. She had made that decision based on evidence. He was the one bringing their relationship into this, when there was really no need. 'You should never have assumed that they would be approved. That was your mistake, not mine.'

'You gave me every indication—'

'I did nothing of the sort,' Meena retorted, sand slipping through her fingers as she searched for any evidence of egg shell. When she had come out here in her boat this morning, she'd had visions of finding hatchlings still in the nest, perhaps unable to find their way out through compacted sand. Now a hollow feeling was growing inside her at the thought that she might have made a mistake. Even a nest full of un-hatched eggs would be something. Something that she could use to prevent the development. But if her fears were correct, and the nest was empty, she would be left with nothing.

'I have maintained throughout this process that the permits would only be granted if you were able to show that the environment around Le Bijou would not be sig-nificantly harmed. You failed to do so. This was the only possible conclusion.' She tried to hide her fears from Guy, tried to hide the worst-case scenario that was playing out under the sand. Until Guy caught her expression.

'What's wrong?' he asked. And then, 'Shouldn't we have found something by now?'

'Yes,' she said shortly, not offering more than that monosyllable as she kept on digging,

But when she finally looked up he fixed her with a stare and she couldn't look away. Because as much as she might be a professional, they both knew that there was more to their relationship than that. She was man-aging to keep that under control, for now. But the lon-ger that she was forced to look at his face, the harder it was to keep memories from her mind. Those early, hazy memories in the private clinic, as a kind nurse had taken her hand and explained about the baby that had slipped away while she had been sleeping.

'What's wrong?' Guy asked, and she knew from

the tenor of the voice that her despair was showing on her face.

She fought to keep the words from her lips, but it was going to be impossible to conceal for ever. The best she could do was get it over and done with. 'There's...there's nothing here. Nothing at all.'

An emptiness opened up inside her as she spoke the words, as she started to accept them.

'What? What does that mean?' Guy asked.

'It must have been a false crawl,' Meena said, finally sitting back on her heels and rubbing the aching muscles in her arm. She stripped off her blue latex gloves and threw them on the sand. 'Sometimes, turtles will crawl up the beach, dig a nest but not lay any eggs. That's what must have happened here.'

'And that means no baby turtles.'

'No hatchlings,' she confirmed. And no hope for a reprieve for Le Bijou. Guy would get her report overturned with her superiors; she knew it. There just wasn't enough to stop the development. Not without the hatchlings.

She nodded, then moved to the blanket that she'd spread out under the shade of a coconut tree, picking up her water bottle and her clipboard. The longer that she stared into that empty nest, the larger the empty feeling inside her grew. She had to get away from it.

Guy came to sit beside her.

'Meena,' he said, the ice melting from his voice. 'Are you okay? We never talked about what happened the last time we were here. I'm sorry that I accused you of letting that interfere with our work. But...'

She couldn't do this now. Couldn't have this conversation. Not with the emotions that seeing that empty nest had brought rushing to the surface. It was more than the loss of the hatchlings she was feeling. It was another loss, another time, when she had felt all the potential of a life to be lived snatched away before it had started. And she couldn't let Guy see those feelings, because it would mean telling him about the miscarriage, and she had already decided that she couldn't do that to him.

'I should have called you,' Guy said. 'To talk about what happened. We shouldn't have left it like that.'

'Or I should have called,' Meena conceded. 'I should have dealt with our personal relationship before I sent you my decision about the permits.'

'Dealt with it?'

She shrugged, choosing her words carefully, not sure in what direction she wanted this conversation to go. 'I should have spoken to you about what happened between us.'

She had barely even let herself think about what she felt about that kiss. The kiss itself she hadn't been able to hide from. It had played in her mind, over and over, since the minute that it had happened. But as for where that left her and Guy? It was safer not to think about it. Not to wonder whether he was thinking of her at all. Whether he was replaying that kiss in agonisingly intense detail, as she had been.

'And what would you have said?' Guy asked, his voice dropping.

Meena held her breath. She didn't know what she

would have said. She still didn't know what she wanted to say. She wanted to say that the kiss had shaken her and grounded her at the same time. That she was terrified and also desperate to do it again. She wanted to ask if that was how it had been before. If there was something between them that had survived her accident—a part of who she had been that summer who was still living in her skin.

But she couldn't say any of that. Because the hard, cold look on his face told her he didn't want to hear a word of it. 'I would have said, I hope we can be adult enough to keep what happened separate from our professional life, and that my decision had nothing to do with what happened that night.'

For the first time since he had walked onto the beach, she saw a crack of warmth in his expression, and she breathed a sigh of relief. 'How am I doing with adulting so far?' he asked with a wry smile.

She grinned in return. 'Not great. Me?'

'Mixed reviews.'

She felt the tension leaching from the atmosphere as they both laughed out loud.

'Maybe we should talk about it, though,' Guy said, his voice taking on a serious tone that made Meena inexplicably nervous.

'What is there to say?' Meena asked, avoiding meeting his eye.

Guy shrugged. 'I think I should apologise. I shouldn't have done it.'

Meena drew her eyebrows together. 'I don't remember it being done to me,' she objected. 'I'm fairly sure I remember joining in.'

Guy shook his head, and she knew that he was shaking off her words too. 'But I knew that I shouldn't be doing it even as it was happening. And so I should apologise.'

Meena swallowed. Just because she had been equally sure that the kiss had been a mistake, that didn't mean that it was any less bruising to her ego to hear it out loud.

'Let's not mention it again, then,' she said, making her voice extra bright to cover her feelings. But still, she was…curious. She knew her own reasons for resisting the urge that had tried to convince her to take that kiss further. The urge that was trying to convince her it was the right thing to lean in and kiss Guy again. But what were his?

He had wanted her. She might be inexperienced, but she had known that much from the second before Guy's lips had touched hers. And he had had feelings for her once. So what had happened in the meantime to make the thought of a relationship with her so abhorrent?

She had broken his heart, she reminded herself, when she hadn't come to Australia to meet him as they had planned. That would be reason enough for him to not want to go over old ground, she was sure. But it seemed like more than that. As if he was hiding something. As if there was something about himself that he didn't want her to see.

'It's probably best,' Guy said. 'What happened between us all those years ago, it's ancient history. There's no need to drag it all back up again. The other night, that was just a…a slip.'

Of the tongue? Meena thought, remembering the English idiom. Interesting choice of words…

Guy's eyes were fixed on her face, and Meena felt suddenly uncomfortable under his gaze, the way that he was studying her and the crease that had just appeared in his forehead.

'What?' she asked, against her better judgement.

'I just don't…' He hesitated but then seemed to come to a decision. 'I don't understand how you knew,' he said. 'How you knew that we had been together before. I did nothing that would give it away.'

Meena fought to keep her expression under control, not to give away anything about how she had known that she'd had a lover that summer. That she'd been looking for him for all the years since. But, with thoughts of the miscarriage so fresh in her mind, it was harder than ever to pretend that it had never happened. 'Well, you might have thought that you hadn't. But you must have done, because I guessed. What other explanation could there be?'

She hoped that she sounded more confident than she felt…

Guy shook his head slowly and she guessed that she hadn't quite pulled it off as well as she had been hoping. 'I don't know,' he said, creasing his forehead once more as he looked at her. 'But I can't shake the feeling that I'm missing something.'

She shook her head in what she hoped was a casual

manner. 'You think I'm keeping secrets?' She felt the blood rush to her face as she asked the question, because of course she was keeping a secret.

She wondered for a moment if she could just tell him about the pregnancy. In the years since it had happened, she had never told anybody. Had never spoken to anyone about it since the nurse who'd first told her that it had happened. She didn't even know if her parents knew about it. They had never said a word if they did. With so much to focus on with her recovery, she'd buried thoughts about the baby as best she could. But, with Guy back in her life, it was suddenly impossible to do that any more, and she couldn't help but think that everything she was thinking must be written on her face.

Guy was watching her through narrowed eyes, and she knew that he suspected that something was wrong. If he had had a sneaking suspicion before that she was keeping secrets from him, then he must be certain of it now.

But she was entitled to secrets, she reminded herself. She didn't owe him her honesty, or anything else, for that matter. He was an associate and nothing more. That kiss on the beach of Le Bijou was a throwback to a different time. It didn't change anything about who they were to each other in the present.

But she felt different from how she had before it had happened, she acknowledged. She couldn't help it. She had wanted that kiss and, now that she knew how good it was to kiss him, to really kiss him, rather than just fantasise about it, she wanted more. And, from the heated look he gave her as he held her eye, she guessed that everything she was thinking was showing on her face.

Guy moistened his bottom lip, and with that tiny movement she was so very nearly lost. Because she knew that he was thinking the same as her. That he could taste her, as she still had the taste of him in her mouth. If she closed her eyes she could feel his hands skimming the curve of her waist, dropping lower, pulling her closer. She could feel the thud of his heart under her hand and hear the rush of blood in her ears as she had abandoned rational thought and let instinct take over.

She closed her eyes for a long moment, took a deep breath, and when she opened her eyes she was in control again. Memories of that night had been banished.

'What happens next?' Guy asked, and for a moment she thought that he was talking about them, and she was almost at the point of telling him that nothing happened next when she realised that he was trying to bring the conversation back to work. That he was talking about the permits. She felt another flush of blood to her face and hoped that Guy hadn't noticed.

'You submit revised plans,' she told him simply, trying to get her mind back into the game. 'Address all of the points in the environmental report and we will reconsider your application. If you meet all the requirements, the permits will be approved.'

His plans *would* probably be approved eventually, she knew. Guy wouldn't stop until they were. And then he expected her to come and work here, to oversee the destruction of the island in the guise of trying to protect it. She had thought that accepting his job offer would be for the best. That Le Bijou needed someone to stand up for it, and she would be the right person. But, with everything that had happened here in the last week, she knew that she couldn't be the person to do it. The memory of their kiss, the fresh raw grief of that empty nest: it was too much.

'Even if they're approved, though, I can't accept your job offer,' Meena added suddenly.

'Excuse me?' Guy said, his head snapping across to look at Meena. Of course he sounded surprised— she was surprised too. She hadn't meant to say it like that. Or say it at all to his face yet. She had planned to send an impersonal email to Dev and then never have to see the look on Guy's face when he heard the news.

She wasn't sure what she was so scared of seeing there. Or maybe it was more a case of what she *wanted* to see there. Did she want him to be disappointed? To be sorry that after she completed her report there was going to be no reason for them ever to talk again? She couldn't read him well enough to know which it was. His face was hard, stony, giving nothing away.

'I thought you were going to take it,' he said, his words calm and measured, giving her no clue to what he was thinking.

'I thought I would too,' she admitted, lifting her shoulders and letting them fall.

'What changed?' he asked, his voice hard.

'I can't,' she said. 'I can't watch that happen to Le Bijou.'

Guy's jaw tensed further, and she knew that he was angry. 'Fine.'

The careful control behind that monosyllable didn't make him seem any less irritated. He couldn't really make it any clearer that it was anything but fine. Well, that was okay with her. She wasn't going to stand here and pretend that she was happy about him destroying the place that she loved more than any other. It wasn't up to her to make him feel better about what he was doing.

'Has it got something to do with the secret that you're keeping?' Guy asked out of nowhere, taking Meena off guard.

'No! And there is no secret!' she said, a little too forcefully, making Guy narrow his eyes at her. Great—she'd made him more suspicious of her. It wasn't fair—her decision genuinely had nothing to do with having lost the baby. But now her over-the-top denial was making her look more suspicious than ever.

'I'm not sure that I believe you,' Guy said, taking a step towards her.

That was fine. She didn't need him to believe her. She just needed him to drop it.

'Never mind,' Guy said at last, when it became clear that she wasn't planning on answering him. 'It's none of my business anyway.'

Her face fell. She knew that her expression was giving her away but she couldn't stop it. Because of all the things that he could have said to her, that was by far the worst. Because of course it was his business. As much as she had tried to put the thought out of her head, it had been his baby that she had lost. If the accident had never happened, it would have been his baby she would have given birth to. Of course that was his business. She had kept the secret, trying to protect him from the hurt that she knew was inevitable. But she wasn't sure any more that that was her decision to make.

'What? What have I said?' Guy asked. 'Is your secret something to do with me, with us?'

She wanted to shake her head and deny it, but there was a difference between lying by omission and lying outright, and it turned out she wasn't actually great at either of them.

'I think you should probably just tell me what's going on,' Guy said, giving her a stern look.

'I don't know how,' Meena admitted, not wanting to look up and meet his gaze. Even after all this time, the pain she felt when she thought about what she had lost felt as fresh as the day she had first found out. How could she inflict that on Guy when she had the choice to spare him?

Was that what she would have wanted? she asked herself. She realised she had never considered the question before. But if she could have woken from her coma with no idea about the life that had once been growing inside her—would she want that?

No.

The answer came to her as quickly as it was decisive. That life had been important. Valuable. And she wouldn't want to diminish that by forgetting. And she owed Guy the same consideration she had been shown.

She sank into a chair, knowing what she had to do, that knowledge making it more impossible than ever to look him in the eye. Before she realised what was happening, Guy was sitting beside her, reaching for her hand, and she wondered what must be showing on her face for his sudden change of mood.

'Is it something I can help with, Meena?' he asked, and she nearly broke at the tenderness in his voice. She shook her head.

'There's nothing you can do. Nothing anyone can do. It's in the past but it still…'

'It still hurts,' Guy said simply, and she nodded. 'It's something to do with when we were together. Or your accident.'

'Yes. Both.'

With gentle fingers, he lifted her chin, forcing her to meet his gaze.

'What is it? You can trust me, Meena.' And she knew that she could. Despite everything, when she was with him she got that same feeling as she did when she was on Le Bijou. A feeling like nothing could touch her. That she was protected from the worst ravages of the real world. She took a deep breath, knowing that nothing was going to happen that would make this any easier. That she couldn't delay any longer.

'I was pregnant, Guy, when the accident happened. I lost your baby.' She watched as his face creased with confusion, then shock and pain, coming to rest firmly on the latter.

'Why didn't you tell me before?' he asked, leaning away from her, subtly putting space between them.

Meena shook her head. 'I thought it would be better for you not to know. I didn't want you to feel the pain that I did.'

His expression registered shock, and she waited for it to shift or change, but it was fixed there, much as she remembered her own world stopping when she had first been told the news. She squeezed his hand, knowing what a blow he had just received. Wanting him to understand that he wasn't alone in this.

'Why did you change your mind?' he asked eventually.

'You had a right to know,' she conceded. 'I finally understood that.'

'I was going to be a father?' he asked, a slight tremor in his voice.

Meena gave a sad smile. 'I think so.'

'You think so?'

She took a deep breath, facing some of the uncertainties that had haunted her the longest. That had made her life the hardest over the years. Exposing the depths to which she had lost her sense of herself when the accident had stolen her memories.

'I know that I was pregnant,' she explained, 'because the doctors in the clinic told me that I had had a miscarriage. But I don't remember it, Guy. I don't remember knowing that I was pregnant—*if* I knew that I was pregnant. I don't know what we would have wanted for the future. I don't know how we would have felt about a baby coming. We weren't married. I was going back to my research...'

He reached for her hand, looking closely at her face as he narrowed his eyes.

'You thought we wouldn't be happy about it?' he asked.

'I... I don't know.' It was just one of the many, many things that she didn't know about that summer. Who she'd been, what she'd wanted. How she'd changed.

'I do,' Guy said, squeezing her hand and moving closer again. 'You would have told me, if you'd known about the baby. I know it. And we would have been excited.' She was sure that his sad smile mirrored her own as they both thought about a life they hadn't lived. A future that had been wrecked out on that road.

'But...?' How could he be so sure? How could he be so sure about what she would have wanted when she didn't even know these things about herself?

'It wouldn't have mattered,' Guy said, and she clung to the certainty in his voice. 'Any of it. We would have been happy.'

She shook her head. 'I can't believe I have to rely on you to tell me how I would have felt. How do I know if you're telling the truth?'

He shrugged. 'I'm sorry. I can't begin to know how difficult that must be. I guess you have to decide whether you can trust me or not. I'm sorry I can't give you more than that.'

She breathed out and realised how much of a relief that was. How long she'd been carrying the fear that, as painful as it was to have lost the baby, perhaps before the accident she hadn't wanted it.

'We'd talked about it,' Guy said, and Meena's eyes widened in surprise.

'But how could we have? You said you didn't know I was pregnant.'

'No, not this baby.' He shook his head and she wondered what he was thinking. Wished that she knew him well enough to guess what he was feeling right now. 'But we had talked about the future,' he went on. 'About children and marriage.'

How had they become so serious in so short a time that a smashed skull could erase it? she wondered, disbelieving. And how could it have ended so abruptly? Both of them going on with their lives as if it had never happened. As if it had never mattered.

'Did you not wonder why I didn't come to Australia?' Meena asked, wanting answers to the questions that had haunted her for seven years.

'Of course I wondered,' Guy snapped, pulling his hand away. 'I called your phone, but no one answered. I emailed. Same. You weren't on social media. I could have called the resort, but you'd been so scared that if anyone found out about us that you would lose your job and I didn't want to risk it. What would you have done, if the situation had been reversed?'

What would she have done? How could she possibly know? She had no idea why she'd made any of the decisions that she had when it came to Guy. No idea about who the woman making those decisions had been.

Except that wasn't really true any more, was it? Not after that night on Le Bijou when she'd started kissing him and never wanted to stop. For the first time, she'd started to understand what had happened that summer. Had started to feel like the woman who had made those decisions.

'I would have tried to find you,' Meena said, but added on a sigh, 'But I'm not sure I could have done more than you did.'

'After a while, I just assumed that you had…moved on. And it made sense, really. Plenty of people have summer romances and they just…end.'

She shook her head. She thought that he'd known her better than that. At least, that was what she'd wanted to believe. 'I don't. I didn't.'

'I know.' He reached for her hand again and she didn't stop him. Didn't want to. She felt anchored, with her hand in his. As if she could start to put the pieces of herself back together again. As if she could finally start to understand herself.

'Can you tell me any more about the baby?' Guy asked, his voice quiet.

Meena took a deep breath. 'I'm so sorry, Guy, but there isn't much to tell. I was only a few weeks pregnant. Barely far enough along to take a test. That's all the doctors were able to tell me when I woke up.'

'So we won't know whether it would have been a boy or a girl.'

She shook her head. 'I'm sorry.'

He squeezed her hand again, and Meena felt it in her chest. 'You don't have to keep apologising,' Guy said. 'It wasn't your fault.'

'Well, it certainly wasn't anyone else's,' Meena

said, voicing a thought she'd always shied away from. 'Whose fault was it, if not mine?'

'How about the person that caused the accident?' Guy asked. 'You know, you've never told me what happened.'

Because there wasn't much to tell, and she'd had it all second-hand anyway. She didn't remember a moment of it. 'It's not much of a story. I was crossing a road and apparently a motorbike came too fast around a corner, lost control and knocked me over. Head injury. Internal injuries. I think you can imagine the rest.'

'How long were you in the clinic?'

'In total? A couple of years.'

She laughed at the surprise on his face; what else could she do? 'Did you think I just got up and walked out? Guy, I had to learn to walk. I had to learn to talk. I was lucky that I had health insurance. If it wasn't for all the support at the clinic, I don't know that I would have ever been able to live independently. I've only been diving again for a year or so. Did you know they make you wait *five years* after a serious head injury? I'm lucky that I haven't suffered from fits since it happened. If I had, I wouldn't have been allowed back in the water at all. I was worried, every day of those five years, that I would never be able to get properly back in the water again.'

'So by the time you got out of the clinic...' Guy started, finally piecing together the timeline of their relationship.

'Everything from that summer was gone. My phone

was destroyed. I couldn't access any of my online ac-
counts for months because I barely knew who I was.
By the time I was even thinking about it, the tech
companies made it impossible and I didn't have the
energy to fight them. I had to let it all go, start fresh,
concentrate on my recovery and rehab.'

'You let me go,' he said sadly.

But it wasn't as simple as that. She hadn't let go,
not really. She hadn't even known what she was cling-
ing to, but she'd never stopped thinking about who the
man she had given herself to might have been. 'I didn't
know who you were. All I knew was that I had been
pregnant. I found a couple of notes, scribbled on the
back of a dive plan, that made me think that maybe I'd
had a boyfriend. They were the only clues that I had.
It wasn't enough to go on.'

'I wish I'd been here.'

She couldn't let herself think about that. About all
the ways that her life might have been different if
his flight had been a week later, or if she'd crossed
the road in a different spot. They could have a family now—could *be* a family now. It was too strange
even to consider.

It still didn't feel like her, the woman who had been
hit by the motorcycle. In a way, Meena was glad that
she couldn't remember that time. Because she didn't
have to think about how much she had changed. What
had motivated that change. She could try to get on with
her life as she had been before her memories had gone.

Until Guy had turned up and reminded her that that
wasn't possible. She couldn't pretend that she hadn't

changed that summer. Even without her memories, she had known that something was different. And that was why she'd spent the last seven years trying to make sense out of the different pieces of her life. And why she had consistently failed. Because she needed to know it all to make sense of it.

She realised with a jolt that her hand was still resting in Guy's, and with another jolt that she had no intention of moving it. Because this was the missing piece. She couldn't figure out who she had been that summer unless she followed through on these feelings that she had for Guy. Unless she acted now, as she had acted then, to see if that made her understand who she had been. She pulled his hand a little closer to her and then looked up, meeting his eye.

He had sat down close to her on the sand. He had taken her hand. But she was the one who was going to move closer. To tip her face up to his and make absolutely clear what she wanted from him.

'Meena…' he started to say, but she laid a hand on his arm and he stopped, his gaze moving from her face down to her hand and then back to her eyes. 'This is not a good idea,' he said eventually.

'Does that mean that you don't want to do it?' she asked, without a hint of guile, because really she just wanted to know that they were on the same page, that she hadn't misread the situation and was about to make a complete fool of herself.

'Of course I want to,' he said, and she thought that it might be the simplest, most uncomplicated thing that he had said to her since he had shown up in St

Antoine. But the consequences of his confession were anything but simple. 'That doesn't mean that I think we should. I'm going to be leaving soon,' he reminded her, as if the thought didn't already haunt her. 'Again.'

'I know that,' she said. 'I'm not looking to the future. But…but my past is so complicated. And so much of it is missing, and I think that… I think that we could fill in some of those gaps, if you wanted…'

He shook his head, spoke softly, one hand coming up to play with the curls that fell forward towards him. 'We can't recreate the past, Meena,' he said. 'I think we've proved that already. It's not going to bring your memories back.'

'I know that,' she said quietly, turning her face towards his hand, where it played gently with her hair. 'I'm coming to terms with that. And I don't want to just re-enact the past either. But I want to understand who I was then. And this is a way to do that.'

'So I'm just an experiment to you. Is that your plan? It's hardly fair to ask that of me, Meena. What do I get out of it?'

She pulled back, taken aback by the bluntness of his question. He looked startled, too, at having asked that.

'I'm sorry,' he said, moving closer as suddenly as he had retreated, the shock falling from his face leaving something softer, yet more intense. 'Stupid question.' His hand lifted to her face, cupping her cheek as he moved closer. So close that she could feel the warmth of his breath on her lips. 'I get you.'

'And that's not enough?' she asked, wishing her voice didn't sound so small.

'God, Meena.' He sounded as if the words were being ripped from his throat. 'It was always enough.'

His hands threaded through her hair, pausing as they encountered the bumps of her scar tissue, smoothing them with his fingertips. He tilted her face back up to his and then his lips were on hers.

That's not enough? He wasn't sure that anything was ever going to be enough when it came to Meena. From before the moment that his lips had touched hers, he'd wanted the wet heat of her mouth. From the instant that he'd felt her tongue against his, he'd wanted more, deeper. When her body pressed against him, he wanted heated, naked skin, cool silk sheets and weeks to rediscover her body.

It had always been that way for him.

When they had first been together, she'd been the one to hold back. To grant first kisses, then touches. And she had held back in other ways, too. She had been the one who had insisted that they keep their relationship a secret. Which he'd understood. Of course he had—St Antoine was a conservative country; women could be judged harshly for sex outside of marriage. And she'd been worried for her job, what might happen if she was found having a relationship with him.

But it had still angered him. Because what did any of it matter, if she was moving to Australia? But she had been insistent that she didn't want to be the subject of gossip, even if she was leaving soon. And she didn't want to be fired—she wanted a letter of recommendation. Which had all been completely reasonable, he could acknowledge now.

But at the time, once he'd got back to Australia, it had only fuelled this idea that he'd imagined it all. Not the kisses. Not the sex. There was no way his imagination was that good. But the rest of it. Their plans for the future. Their intimacy. The whispered words of love that they had shared, first shyly and then urgently, as his time on the island had drawn to a close and they had realised that they had a decision to make.

Now he knew that she would have come with him if it hadn't been for the accident... And that all his feelings of abandonment and hurt that he had carried with him for years had come from nowhere—or, probably more accurately, from his own fears and insecurities; they had nothing to do with how Meena had felt about him and everything to do with how he had felt about himself. He'd turned that self-doubt against himself, and it had done so much damage to his heart that the pain had radiated out and started to hurt the people around him. But the damage had been done, whether it was based on a misunderstanding or not. And he couldn't risk hurting Meena again.

She'd been through too much. Deserved better than him. Better than the person who he was now.

But, when he was kissing her, he didn't feel like that person any more.

He felt again like the man he had been when he had first met her. When he'd been trying to find a way to impress his parents, getting to know their business and hoping that they would see that he wasn't as useless as they seemed to think. Like a man who had found the person who made him feel strong, capable and decisive.

Meena moaned into his mouth, and he didn't care whether he was the boy he had been before or the man he was now. All he knew was that he was a man, and the woman he desired more than any other was kissing him back, and he wasn't going to stop her.

How could he stop her, when this was everything that he wanted? With Meena in his arms, sliding onto his lap, he could believe that he was wrong. That he could be the person who fell in love with her again. That he could love her without hurting her.

Meena's hands tightened on his shoulders and he wrapped his arms round her waist in response, rolling over so he was lying above her, the sun hot on the back of his head, her body soft beneath him. Her shirt had rucked up as he'd rolled them over and he couldn't resist the heat of that golden-bronze skin. His hand explored, and his eyes and lips followed, her fingers threading through his hair as he pressed first one kiss and then another to the soft skin of her stomach.

But then with a wrench she pulled her shirt down, and he lifted himself up on his elbows, looking into Meena's eyes as she lay beneath him.

Which was enough time for doubt to flicker over her features.

'Guy… I can't,' she said. 'This isn't me.'

His brows creased. 'I don't want to do anything you don't want to, Meena,' he said, putting more space between them. 'But…if this is what you want… Meena, it *is* you. It can *be* you.'

'But I don't do this sort of thing,' she said, wrapping her arms around her body.

He gave her a small smile. 'It doesn't have to be a *sort of thing* you do,' Guy said, giving her space, but looking at her so intensely that she felt herself squirm. 'It can just be something that you want to do now. Here. With me.'

He moved away from her a fraction more, leaving her cold where he had been pressed against her. She relaxed a little, secure in the knowledge that if she didn't want this then he wouldn't want it either. This would be so much easier if she actually knew what she wanted, though.

Except that wasn't right, she acknowledged to herself. She knew exactly what she wanted. What she wanted was laid out in front of her, waiting for her to come to him. The question was whether she was going to take it. She wanted him, but she couldn't shake that voice in her head that told her that she shouldn't.

Guy leaned towards her and kissed her lips so softly, so gently, that she felt herself melting. And with that, she knew that this couldn't be wrong. It didn't matter what she'd thought she'd had planned for her life. All she had to think about was what she wanted for herself now. And she knew that there was no way that this could be anything other than beautiful.

She kissed him back, her lips curving into a smile.

'Is this okay?' Guy asked breathlessly between kisses.

'Very okay,' she whispered back. This time it was her hands that went exploring, skimming over his skin, tracing out the shape of his shoulder blades, the bumps of his spine down the centre of his muscled back.

She had never imagined that she could want this so much. That she could want more—but she did. She couldn't imagine anything any more that would make her want to stop touching Guy, that would stop her wanting him to touch her. Guy's hands had stilled when she had drawn away before, but she wanted his fingers back on her skin, showing her everything that he had once known about her body. Things that she herself couldn't remember.

She reached down for the hem of her shirt and pulled it over her head. She soaked in the desire in Guy's eyes for a moment as he drank in the sight of her, and she was amazed by how powerful that made her feel. How intoxicating that feeling was. And then his eyes dropped to the scars that criss-crossed her stomach and she tensed.

'From the accident,' he murmured. It was more a statement than a question as he traced one scar from the curve of her waist down towards her navel and the waistband of her shorts.

She bit her lip and nodded. 'Uh-huh,' she muttered, not capable of forming words.

'I'm so sorry,' Guy said, dipping his forehead to rest on hers, his fingers never stilling on that scar, tracing up and down, up and so slowly down. 'I wish I had been here,' he said, and Meena held her breath, because how different would her life have been if that had been the case? 'I would have kissed these better,' he whispered, and then the sun was dazzlingly bright in her eyes as his head dipped lower, kissing her neck, collarbone, then the soft curve of her belly, his lips replacing his fingers, tracing over the bumps of her scars, lower and lower and lower.

CHAPTER TEN

HER BODY HAD never felt so heavy. Her limbs were jelly; her eyelids were a rockfall across the entrance of a cave. Who cared? Meena thought. She didn't need to move. To see. She'd just exist here, with the sun heating her skin and Guy's breath still stuttering in her ear.

She groaned as he rolled away from her, but he grabbed her hand and squeezed, then pulled her closer, so she was tucked under his arm, her cheek pressed against the hot, damp skin of his chest.

So, finally, she understood.

This was who she had been that summer she had first met Guy. *This* was why she had made the decisions she had. And this was how she had got pregnant. Because the pull of this was irresistible and, now that she knew these sensations existed, she wasn't entirely sure how she was going to get anything done ever again.

And yet, the feelings weren't entirely new. There was something comfortingly familiar about the warm heaviness that weighed down her limbs. About the way that her body and Guy's fitted together. There was something so right about being tucked up beside him that made her think that perhaps her body remembered him, even if her brain didn't.

It made her wonder if her memories were still in there somewhere, just waiting for her to find the right route back to them. But perhaps they weren't, and for the first time that thought didn't frighten her. Frankly, how could she care if it meant that she got all these firsts again? First kiss. First love...

She smiled, listening to the gentle crash of the waves, soaking in the rays of the sun filtered by the coconut trees swaying above them. Grateful for the touch of a gentle breeze over her damp skin. She couldn't imagine anything more perfect.

Couldn't imagine a memory that she would choose over this one.

And that was when it hit her. Any day now, this perfect scene would be destroyed when the builders moved in and started to dig up this island. All because Guy wanted to destroy the place that had been so special to them. She shuddered as real life filtered through her fantasy. She couldn't lie on his chest any more with that knowledge burning through her. And she couldn't even look at him.

So now she *really* knew. Knew what it was like to be so blinded by her desire for Guy that all sense was forgotten. Knowing that she'd repeated the same stupid mistakes she'd made when she'd been much younger and more naïve burned in her chest. She pushed herself upright, looking around for her clothes, scrambling into her shirt and underwear.

Guy pushed himself up on his elbows, his expression the definition of confusion. 'Meena?' he said, watching her battle with her clothes in a belated attempt at dignity. 'What's wrong?' he asked, his eyes narrowing as he took in the change in atmosphere.

'Everything,' Meena replied. 'This is wrong. A mistake. We never should have...'

'I don't understand what just happened,' he said, pulling on his shorts while Meena gathered up the blanket, her papers and started throwing everything into her bag.

'What just happened is I realised I've made a huge mistake.'

Guy frowned. 'Is there any way to take that other than as an insult?'

'Probably not,' she conceded, keeping her focus on tidying their things rather than seeing the censure she knew must be waiting for her if she looked at Guy.

'Are you going to explain it, then?' he demanded.

'I don't believe I have to, Guy. You already know—you want to destroy this island. The only reason you were here in the first place was to try to make sure that I approve your environmental report and help make that happen. I can't believe that I forgot that, even for a second.'

He stood watching her in silence, and any hope that they could somehow rescue this situation fled. There was no way around it. She would do anything to protect this island. He would do anything to destroy it. That had been the situation when he had first walked onto this beach and found her flat on her back on the sand,

and nothing had changed since then. The fact that she had fallen for him somewhere along the way—again— meant nothing. It meant less than nothing.

'If that's the way you feel,' Guy said, every word a violent slash at her heart. It wasn't the way that she felt. It was the truth. It was his truth. 'I should go.'

'You probably should,' she agreed. 'Get your revised plans to me by the end of the week. I'm sure we can find a way to put the application through, now that we know the nest was empty.'

He stopped and looked at her.

'Is that what this is really about? The turtles?'

'It's all the same thing, Guy. This is about Le Bijou, and the fact that I would do anything to protect it.'

'Including sleeping with me?'

She whipped her head round to stare at him, open-mouthed. 'Are you really going to accuse me of that, Guy?' she asked. 'You think I would do this to try and change your mind? Well, thank you for proving me right. This *was* a mistake. I barely know you. And you've just proved you don't know me at all. I thought you understood that this was special to me.'

He had the grace to look ashamed, at least. But it didn't make his words go away. They couldn't be unsaid. 'I know that.' He took a step towards her, but seemed to think better of it. 'I'm sorry, Meena. I didn't really believe that you would do that.'

'But you said it.'

'And I take responsibility for that. But I want you to know that I truly don't believe it.'

'Fine. I understand. Now, I think we should get off this island.'

She looked over at where her boat was tied up on the rickety old dock, glad that they had arranged to arrive separately. The last thing that she wanted was to be trapped in close confines with him for a moment longer. But, when they got to the jetty, Guy jumped down into her boat rather than into the cockpit of his speedboat.

CHAPTER ELEVEN

WHY HAD HE said it? The only answer he could give himself was that he had wanted to hurt Meena. He hadn't believed what he had said, so what other answer could there be?

Which proved that she had the right idea, ignoring what had just happened between them and resuming their former hostilities. Meena was right. He wasn't going to change his mind about Le Bijou. How could he?

But he wanted to. The voice at the back of his mind was too loud to be ignored now. He had wanted to build this development to erase Meena from his memories, but he realised now how impossible that would be. Even if every grain of sand on this island were removed, Le Bijou was soaked in Meena and in memories of their time here. There wasn't enough concrete in the world that could make him forget her. Instead, he had made things worse. Made new memories, which were all the more unbearable for their freshness.

And he had hurt Meena. Over and over this afternoon, he had hurt her without even meaning to, trying to. He had hurt her when he had made love to her with no thoughts for the future, and no intention of dropping his plans for his development. He had hurt her when he had accused her of sleeping with him to push her own agenda, rather than...

Rather than what? He realised he had been so quick with his accusation, hurt at the way Meena had suddenly cooled towards him, that he hadn't considered why she *had* slept with him. Or why he had slept with her, for that matter.

It was because he had wanted her so much he could barely breathe, he acknowledged to himself. He had wanted her as fiercely now as he ever had when they'd been younger. And he'd seen that same desire in her. Seen it overcome her hesitation and reserve.

He had loved her once. But that love had twisted and soured in him until he was the man he was now—incapable of having a relationship with a woman without hurting her. They had gone from perfection to disaster in the space of a breath, and he had no idea how.

But he knew now, more than ever before, that his decision to stay well away from relationships was the right one. How could he choose anything else, knowing what happened to the women that he got involved with? Thank goodness Meena had seen sense while they'd been lying on the sand on Le Bijou, because he wasn't sure that he would have had the strength to end it if she hadn't.

Being with Meena again was everything that he had dreamed about almost every night since he had last known her. But he knew that it couldn't happen again. That he couldn't risk hurting her again.

'I don't want to leave things like this,' he said as Meena stashed her bags in the storage locker, the side of the boat bumping against the jetty as it rocked under their weight. Meena kept her eyes on what she was doing, though he had to wonder why it was taking her so long. She was avoiding speaking to him, of course. The answer was as obvious as it was unwelcome. Because now he had to say goodbye. Again.

He had no doubt that Meena would make sure that they didn't meet again. She had all the information she needed for the environmental report. The turtle nest had been the last hurdle in the way of his development, and when she had excavated it and found it empty all his concerns should have fallen away as that final hurdle was cleared. Instead, all he could see was the grief that had creased Meena's face as she had realised that there were no eggs.

He wasn't sure which was worse for her. The loss of her fight against the development, or the reminder of the baby she had lost. But the pain had been raw and tangible.

The miscarriage hadn't been just 'her' loss, though, he acknowledged. It was his too. With everything else that had happened in the last few hours, he had barely had a chance to process that information. She'd been carrying his child when he had left St Antoine. Even though he hadn't known about the baby until it was already too late, he felt a wave of sadness for what might have been. Because he and Meena would have loved that baby. If he hadn't left, if Meena hadn't been struck by that motorbike, then they would be a family now. He could picture it as clearly as if it was real, and the loss of that life struck him with a painful intensity. His knees buckled and he sat on the edge of the boat with a heavy thump, feeling it rock beneath him.

At the sudden motion, Meena turned her head. 'Guy? What is it?' she asked, her expression so concerned that he wondered what was showing on his face.

'Nothing…' he said, but then hesitated. Because, if he left now, he was sure that he would never see her again. And if he never saw her again then who could he possibly talk to about the child and the future that they had lost? She was the only other person on the planet who shared this loss. Who could understand the alternative reality he was grieving for.

'I was thinking about the baby,' he admitted, and her face softened. 'I can't believe I never knew about it.'

'I guess we have that in common,' Meena said, coming to sit beside him. And he could see her point. He had never realised before that he had lost so much when Meena had lost her memories. So much of what they shared, what was important to them, was stored in one or other of their brains, each a backup for the other, and when half their collective memory had been wiped clean they'd both been left incomplete.

Meena, her hands tucked between her knees, her shoulders sloped as she stared down at the deck, said, 'It's only natural to think about it.' And for a moment, she looked as if she didn't hate him. And that lit up something inside him. Something he wanted to nurture, to keep alight.

'I'm glad you told me,' he said, realising suddenly that she had had a choice about that. She could have kept him in the dark and he would have lived his whole life never knowing about the baby they had made together.

'I wasn't sure whether I should,' Meena said in a small voice. 'It hurts so much, to think about it, and I thought I was sparing you that. But then when I excavated that nest...'

'I know,' he said, reaching for her hand and squeezing. 'I know how hard that was for you.'

He told himself that he shouldn't be doing this. That he shouldn't be reaching out to touch her, and the sensible part of his brain agreed completely. But the woman that he had once loved was beside him, hurting, and every part of his body ached to make that better. Holding her hand wasn't much, but it was solidarity. It was telling her that she wasn't the only one who had to carry those memories any more. That they would share this sadness and bear it together.

'I'm glad that you know,' she said at last, her hand still soft in his. He was waiting, he realised, for her to stiffen and pull away, and God knew that was what he deserved after the things that he had said. After what he was trying to do to the island that she loved. But for some reason he couldn't fathom, she wasn't pulling away. Instead her body was leaning closer; and her head had landed soft and warm on his shoulder.

'You've never spoken to anyone about it before?'

She shook her head. 'I couldn't. Not without knowing the full story. Not without being able to tell my parents or my friends who the father was.'

'Well, you're not alone in it any more,' he murmured, risking pressing his cheek to the top of her head. Waiting for her to pull away from him, to realise that she was making a mistake. Putting herself at risk of being hurt. Instead he felt her soften more, her head growing heavier on his shoulder, the weight of her body pressing warmer at his side.

He should be the one to do it, he knew. He wanted to protect her, and the best way that he knew to do that was to stay as far away from her as possible. But he wasn't sure that he could do it any more. He couldn't willingly put more than a breath of space between them. He'd spent every minute since he had arrived here and seen her again for the first time trying to resist her. It had made absolutely zero difference to the way that he felt about her, and he feared he didn't have the strength to keep going.

But she had to know what she was getting into. He was laying everything on the table and had no doubt it would send her running.

'I'm not good for you, Meena,' he said. He waited a moment for the words to sink in, waiting for her to pull away, but she still didn't.

'I don't think I believe that,' she said at last. 'If what you've told me is true, then the Meena who knew you before thought that you were. And I'm learning to trust her judgement.'

He let out a sigh. 'She knew a different me. It was a long time ago.'

'I'm not sure people change that much,' Meena said with a small shrug against his body. 'I think we might be proof of that. Neither of us planned this, or expected it. And yet here we are. Again.'

'I mean it, Meena,' Guy said, sitting up a little straighter, trying to break the intimacy between them. 'I've done things in the last seven years that I'm ashamed of. I've hurt people. People have died. I don't deserve you.'

She looked up at that, meeting his gaze with narrowed eyes.

'Someone died? You hurt them on purpose?' she asked, wary.

He sighed. It was always the wrong question. 'No. Not on purpose, but that doesn't mean that it wasn't my fault. I should have been able to save her. I just… couldn't. I was so wrapped up in my own problems…'

Which made it sound less bad than it had really been. If he had taken better care of Charlotte, if he had at least been with her when she'd taken those pills instead of passed out drunk at home, he could have done *something*. The fact that the damage he'd caused hadn't been intentional didn't absolve him. He should have known better than to get involved with someone when he was still so broken after Meena.

'Guy, you're scaring me. I need you to tell me what happened. Who died?'

He shook his head, unable to believe that he was going to have to tell her this. 'My girlfriend,' he said, trying to keep his voice light. 'The girl I started see-ing after I got back to Australia.'

'How did she die?' Meena asked, her frank gaze giving him nowhere to hide.

He shook his head, covering his eyes. He wished he didn't have to do this, but Meena needed to know. 'She took some pills in a club. I was meant to be there with her, but I'd passed out at home and never made it. If I'd been there, I would have seen that something was wrong. I would have gotten her help sooner. I know it.'

Meena went silent for a moment after he spoke, and he wasn't sure he wanted to know what she was thinking.

'You didn't give her the pills?' she asked, a crease appearing between her eyebrows.

His eyes snapped to hers. 'Of course not.'

'And you didn't make her take them?'

He shook his head. 'No. I didn't want her to take pills. I'd told her before that I didn't like it.'

Meena shook her head. 'Then I don't see how you can think that this is your fault.'

'Because I should have been there with her!' Guy burst out, emotion making his words sharp. 'Charlotte shouldn't have been alone in some disgusting toilet of a dodgy club. If I'd been there with her, I would have got her help sooner. If I'd been able to control my own drinking, control my own feelings…'

'You drank a lot?' Meena asked. 'After you got back to Australia?'

He nodded. 'I thought it would help.'

'Did it?'

'Of course it didn't. And then Charlotte died and everything was so much worse.'

'It wasn't your fault, Guy.' Meena said the words gently, dropping her head and forcing him to meet her eyes. 'You're a good man. You deserve to be happy.'

'I'm not sure I have it in me, Meena. After I left here, and you didn't come, my heart broke—I broke. I tried to start again. But it didn't matter how much I tried. Because I could never feel it. It was never the same. Never real. And so I drank to try and convince myself that it didn't hurt. Charlotte died, and it was a tragedy. But it wasn't the same as losing you. Nothing was real, after you.'

She fell quiet, and it wasn't until he finally looked up and saw her face that she said, 'This feels pretty real.'

'This isn't love,' he said, shaking his head. It couldn't be. Because the implications of that were just too frightening to consider.

'Right.' She edged away from him slightly, caution making her wrap her arms around herself. He hated that he had sent her into self-protection mode. But it was for the best. She *should* be on her guard around him.

'See! I'm doing it already,' he pointed out.

'I'm annoyed, Guy. Not heartbroken.' She sat up a little straighter now, pinning him with a glare before she continued. 'So, let me be sure I have this right. Because someone sold your girlfriend dodgy drugs, and she died due to events beyond either of your control, you've decided you're incapable of having a relation-ship.' Guy nodded. 'That sounds pretty stupid to me.'

'Well, thanks for your understanding,' he said, cross-ing his arms and standing. 'But it doesn't feel stupid from where I'm standing. I don't like hurting people, Meena, but I've been hurting you since the moment I arrived here.'

'Do you want me to hate you?' Meena asked, stand-ing up to face him.

Why couldn't she just take his word that this was a bad idea? *Because if she was the sort of person who didn't question what she was told you wouldn't have fallen in love with her in the first place*, his brain told him, providing the inconvenient answer.

'Of course I don't want you to hate me,' he said.

'Right, I'm the one who decides whether I do, and I don't, as it happens.' She crossed her arms and planted her feet firmly against the slight jostling of the boat and he knew that he was getting nowhere.

'Well, you should,' he repeated, though with dimin-ishing expectations of her taking any notice of what he was trying to tell her.

'I think that says more about how you feel than how I do,' Meena suggested, her posture softening slightly, one hand reaching to touch his arm. 'Why should I hate you, Guy? Because we disagree about the future of Le Bijou? I never expected you to change your mind about that. Not really. Not even when we made love. It was just more convenient for me to…not think about it. I won't let you take sole responsibility for the mistakes we both made. I'm sorry if I made you think that I hate you, because I don't.'

He shook his head. Why wouldn't she just believe him when he said that he didn't deserve her? 'Please, Meena. Just take my word when I say you're better off without me in your life.'

'Honestly, I don't know, Guy. What happened between us was so... I'm not sure I have the words to describe it. And knowing what's going to happen to Le Bijou makes having those feelings difficult for me. But, after everything that you've just told me, I'm not sure that running from them is such a great idea either. You've spent seven years feeling broken from what we had before, from what happened to you after you left here. I feel like there's more to be said. More to talk about. If we both walk away now, then everything is just as broken as it was before. We have a chance to put that right.'

'And I've told you that those chances always end up in someone getting hurt.' His shoulders stiffened beneath her cheek.

'This is different.'

'How?' he asked.

Meena sighed. 'Because we are having this conversation. Have you ever told anyone else what you told me?'

'No.'

'Then I doubt anyone has told you what I'm about to. It wasn't your fault, Guy.' She squeezed his hand and he tried so hard to believe her. 'And what we have is different to what came before. I don't think I've ever

stopped loving you. And if you felt the same way...
maybe you weren't broken, Guy,' she said. 'You aren't.
Maybe things were just...unfinished. And now we can
finish them. One way or the other.'

He shook his head. 'I don't think what we did today
helped things feel more finished, if I'm honest.'

'I know.'

She looked so bloody confused about that that he felt
terrible for pushing this. For making this about him,
when she was the one who had just taken a life-changing
gamble on him. She had chosen him to be her first—
again—and he had let her down—again. And he was
kidding himself if he thought that what had happened
today hadn't been life-changing for him too. Because
there was no coming back from what had happened on
the beach. Already he was thinking differently. Wishing differently. Trying to find a way that they could
give their relationship a second chance. But he knew
that it would be selfish. That any sort of relationship
with Meena risked her getting hurt, and he couldn't be
responsible for that.

He was so sure, Meena thought, watching Guy. So sure
that he knew what was best for her. So sure that his
history was going to repeat itself and that there was
nothing he could do to stop it.

Well, he didn't know the future. And it was time
to prove that to him.

'I never got the chance to tell you, Guy, that I'm
leaving St Antoine.'

The pure shock on his face gave her a tiny buzz of

pleasure. He was so sure that he could predict what was going to happen between them that it pleased her that she could wrong-foot him like that. She wasn't even sure why it was that important to her. But she absolutely knew that she didn't want him writing off her options.

'You're leaving? Why?'

'I decided it was time to get back to my research. I had a position at my old university that I couldn't take up after my accident. There are still opportunities for me there.'

'You're moving back to Australia?'

'That's the plan. And it's one of the reasons why I couldn't accept your job offer.'

'I thought that was because you didn't approve of my plans,' Guy said.

'I didn't. I don't. But that wasn't the only factor. Meeting you again has shown me how much I've put my life on hold. I've been obsessed with getting my memories back. Trying to work out who I was that summer. And I'm starting to understand that it's really not that important. Or, at least, it's not the most important thing. What's important is who I am now. What I want to do next.'

'But you don't have to leave to do that. If this is because of me, because of what I'm doing at Le Bijou, I'll drop it, Meena. I'll find a way to stop it.'

She stared at him, open-mouthed. 'You'd do that? To stop me moving to Australia? You've said all along that there's nothing you can do to stop the development. But now I'm talking about moving to the same country as you and suddenly you can find a way? Were you lying before or are you lying now?'

'What? No, it's not because we'd be in the same country. And I haven't lied. But I don't want to be responsible for you having to leave. I know how much you love St Antoine and Le Bijou. I can't have that on my conscience too.'

'You knew before how much I loved it. You weren't too concerned about your conscience then.'

'I did know it, but… I don't know. The thought of you having to leave here because of what I've done… I've hurt so many people already, Meena. I'm not sure I can handle that too.'

She was still staring, and he started to shift uncomfortably. Of all the reactions he could have predicted, anger hadn't been high on the list.

'How many times do I have to say it, Guy?' she went on. 'I'm choosing this. Me. This isn't something that you're doing to me. It isn't about you at all. This is something that I want, for myself. Can't you credit me with that? Not everything that I do has to be about you. And, if you're worried I'm going to be too close just because we happen to be sharing the same continent, don't worry. I'm still going to be two thousand kilometres away. I don't think you have to worry about bumping into me at the supermarket.'

'That's not what I was worried about,' he said, shaking his head.

'Good. That's settled, then,' Meena said, crossing her arms and willing him off her boat.

'I don't feel like anything's settled,' Guy countered,

making no move to jump back on the jetty. 'I feel like things are getting more confusing by the minute, Meena. I just told you that I'd cancel my development. I thought that was what you wanted.'

'I heard you. And you know already that it's what I want. But honestly, I don't know what to think any more. You weren't prepared to change your plans even when we made love. What's changed now?'

What had changed? He wasn't even sure he understood it himself, never mind being capable of explaining it to someone else. But something had changed. And it wasn't just that he'd told her that he could cancel his plans for Le Bijou, though that was part of it. It was why he'd done it. He'd been so horrified at the thought that he'd be driving her from her home, when she'd already lost so much, that he'd have done anything to right that wrong.

It was the realisation that he was still in love with her. He had to be, because nothing short of that would have made him change his plans. He'd spent years telling himself that he couldn't be in a relationship. That he was too damaged from what had happened with Meena. But what if he wasn't damaged? What if Charlotte hadn't died because he wasn't a good enough boyfriend? What if it had been nothing more than a tragic accident? Could he really let go of the guilt he had been carrying around for so long?

That would mean that he wasn't broken. That it wasn't impossible for him to have another relationship. That maybe he and Meena *could* try again, and see if they could make it work this time.

Yes, they would still be two thousand kilometres apart if she went back to her old university. But that kind of distance wasn't insurmountable. Not when you were your own boss and had money to throw at the situation. They could make the distance work.

If they wanted to.

And there was the crux of the matter. Would Meena want to? They'd talked round and round and round the issue without either of them facing it head-on. And if he wanted that to change—wanted his future to change—he knew that he was going to have to step up and make it happen.

'I'm killing the development on Le Bijou,' he said, and breathed a sigh of relief after the words were finally out. 'Whatever happens, Meena, I want you to know that. I started the project for all the wrong reasons, and I want to stop it now for all the right ones. I don't want anything to happen to that place. I wanted to destroy it, and all the memories it held for me. And I don't want that any more.'

'I'm glad to hear it,' Meena said cautiously. 'Though it doesn't change my plans.'

'I know. I don't expect it to. But there's something else I need to tell you. I love you, Meena. I never stopped loving you. And I can't believe it's taken me so long to realise how I feel, because my heart has been aching for you since the day that I left St Antoine. I should have grabbed you up the moment that I came back and done everything in my power to try and get you to fall in love with me again. I didn't because I was an idiot, and because I was so sure that I was wrong for you. But now...'

'Now?'

'Now I think I got that wrong. That all I ever wanted was a chance to love you.'

'And, if I gave you that chance, how would this work?'

'It works however you want it to work, Meena. It works in Sydney, or it works here, or on your campus in Queensland. I don't care where we are. I just want a chance.'

CHAPTER TWELVE

A CHANCE. That was all that he wanted. And now it all came down to this—what did she want for her future? Meena had spent so long thinking about her past, agonising over the decisions she didn't even remember making, that she had put off thinking about her future. She'd made one big decision already—that she was ready to get back to her academic career. She'd been so overwhelmed by the knowledge of her past that she'd never even let herself think about her romantic future, but here it was looking her in the face, asking her to take a leap.

Could she trust him? Yes. The answer came to her without deliberation. Even without the change to his plans for Le Bijou she trusted him. She loved him. And if he truly meant what he'd said about changing his mind, then there was nothing standing in their way.

He said that he'd never stopped loving her, and from the heartfelt expression he was wearing, she had no choice but to believe him. He'd been torturing himself over the tragic death of his girlfriend, unable to see that he wasn't responsible, no matter how terrible he felt about it.

She knew that she loved him, too. She had known it the moment she had learned about their history, and the uncanny emotions that she'd felt at seeing him again had suddenly made sense. Of course she still loved him. Her body had never forgotten him, and she was sure that somewhere in the recesses of her brain those precious memories of their summer together were locked away safe.

'I love you, Guy.'

He'd tried to scare her off with his failed romantic history, but none of that mattered. They were both bringing baggage into this relationship, but it didn't matter. Because at last they were being honest with each other, and she was convinced that there was nothing that they couldn't face if they did it together.

'We're going to make this work,' she added as she saw his smile grow. 'If we both want this, we'll find a way for the geography to work. And I *do* want this. I've wanted it since the minute I opened my eyes on Le Bijou and saw you, if I'm honest. Long before I knew what you meant to me.'

'And I've wanted it since the day I left you there, looking just the same as I found you. Lying beneath the coconut and filao trees, eyes closed, just soaking in our favourite place.'

'I don't want you to resent me for making you change your mind about Le Bijou,' she said in a softer voice, concern clouding her expression.

'Meena, I promise you, I will never resent you. This

whole project was about forgetting you. Because I was an idiot. I don't want to forget a second that we spend together. I want us both to treasure those memories. And the ones that you've lost, I'll treasure them enough for the both of us.'

She smiled at that.

'And we'll look after Le Bijou together,' Guy went on. 'And make sure it is always protected. And maybe, one day, we'll bring our family here to enjoy it with us.'

'Our family?'

He nodded and pressed a gentle kiss to her lips. 'It's what I want, Meena. It's what I wanted that summer, and what I've been grieving for ever since. If it's what you want too, then we can make it real.'

'And the distance?' she asked. 'Even when we're both in Australia?'

'It's nothing,' Guy said confidently. 'You're the one who said it. I have a plane. And a helicopter. If you want our home to be in Queensland, I will fly back to you every night.'

'Hardly the environmentally friendly solution...' she replied, eyebrows raised.

'Then I will work remotely. Or I'll move the whole bloody office to Queensland if I have to. I don't care, Meena. I'll make it work, if you just tell me that you want me to.'

She said nothing. For seconds. For days. For long enough that he was convinced that she had changed her mind. Until her face broke out into the beaming smile he'd not seen for seven years, and he knew.

'I want you too.'

She squealed as he wrapped his arms around her waist and lifted her up, the boat rocking beneath them until he had to reach out a hand to steady them. As she slipped down his body, held tight against his chest, he knew that, whatever happened, he wouldn't let her go again.

'I love you, Meena,' he said, half under his breath as he leaned in to kiss her. When her arms wrapped around his neck he finally felt it fall away—the heartache and the grief that he had carried for the last seven years. With her in his arms, he was whole again.

'I love you too,' Meena said, returning his kiss with a freedom and a passion she never remembered feeling before. 'We haven't taken the easy way here,' she added eventually when Guy's arms had loosened to a comfortable weight around her waist and her cheek had found a spot to rest on his breastbone.

'I don't care how we got here,' Guy murmured into her hair, tightening his arms around her for a second. 'I just care that we did. I'm glad that I'm old enough and wise enough to know that I would give anything for this, for you.'

Meena looked up at Guy, at the heartfelt love in his expression, and smiled. 'All you have to give me is yourself.'

'Well, that,' Guy said between kisses, 'is easy. You have me. You've always had me.'

* * * * *

LET'S TALK

Romance

For exclusive extracts, competitions
and special offers, find us online:

f facebook.com/millsandboon

○ @millsandboonuk

𝕐 @millsandboon

Or get in touch on 0844 844 1351*

For all the latest titles coming soon,
visit millsandboon.co.uk/nextmonth

Want even more
ROMANCE?

Join our bookclub today!

'Mills & Boon books, the perfect way to escape for an hour or so.'

Miss W. Dyer

'Excellent service, promptly delivered and very good subscription choices.'

Miss A. Pearson

'You get fantastic special offers and the chance to get books before they hit the shops'

Mrs V. Hall

Visit millsandbook.co.uk/Bookclub and save on brand new books.

MILLS & BOON